A Prisoner of Hope

From Crime to Christ, a series by Rick Conner

A Prisoner of Hope

By
Darron Shipe
Written by
Rick Conner

Writers Club Press
San Jose New York Lincoln Shanghai

A Prisoner of Hope

Writers Club Press
an imprint of iUniverse.com, Inc.

For information address:
iUniverse.com, Inc.
5220 S 16th, Ste. 200
Lincoln, NE 68512
www.iuniverse.com

ISBN: 0-595-15987-7

Printed in the United States of America

Dedication

To all the moms who fall asleep each night crying for their sons and daughters in prison; and to the youth at Bon Air Juvenile Correctional Center who inspired me to write this story.

"As for you, because of the blood of my covenant with you, I will free your prisoners from the waterless pit. Return to your fortress, O prisoner of hope; even now I announce that I will restore twice as much to you."

Zechariah 9:11_12 NIV

INTRODUCTION

If any one would had told me years ago, when I experience my own miracle of transformation, what I know today, and see happening through our ministry, it would had been hard to believe. Its been twenty-nine years since we came to Richmond, Virginia and started New Life For Youth. Throughout the years, we have seen one miracle after another of God's saving grace. Scores of young men and women have come seeking hope and a new beginning for their broken lives. I'm often asked if these men and women who have lived a lifetime of crime and addiction, then spend a year in New Life For Youth, really change. Does it stick? Can they become honorable people in today's society? ABSOLUTELY, YES! The story of Darron Shipe, *A Prisoner of Hope*, is living proof of the cure that comes when a man has an encounter with Jesus Christ. Darron's testimony will take you from the brink of self destruction, a life consumed by drug addiction, hate and violence, to the hope of the gospel of Christ. Darron is a model of the hundreds that have been helped through New Life For Youth. Today, Darron is a man of God, a husband, a father, and a successful businessman in our community. Together with his godly wife, Barbara and their children, they work with us hand in hand in our church, and through their own ministry reaching out to other young people that are trapped just as he was at one time. They preach hope to the hopeless, and salvation to the lost. I highly recommend this book written by a son in the faith whom I have seen transformed by God.

Victor Torres

Senior Pastor of New Life Outreach Intl. Church
Founder of New Life For Youth
Author of *Son of Evil Street*

ACKNOWLEDGMENT

Special thanks to Betty Conner and Addie Gomes for editing, suggestions and advice. Also, Betty Robertson of Creative Christian Ministries for editorial work and priceless wisdom. Their invaluable and sensitive spiritual understanding of evangelism made this book possible.

CHAPTER 1

At one hundred-fifteen miles per hour, the red needle laid buried in the right corner of the dashboard. The stolen 1983 Buick Electra was cream colored with tan leather seats, and had all the buttons and whistles you'd expect from a high dollar car. I loved the way it handled; a steady, solid ride with little sway when weaving in and out of traffic.

Dinky, who was twenty but looked sixteen, was in the front seat. Shenean, her sister, preferred riding in the back. From the corner of my eye, I caught a glimpse of Dinky watching the cars scattering on the road ahead to clear a path. Her eyes bulged with fear as she saw the eight Virginia State Police cars trailing us with blue lights flashing and sirens blaring.

Personally, it had little effect on me. I had little to lose with a parole violation and thirteen felony warrants hanging over my head from Maryland. I knew I was going back to prison if we got caught. The parole violation alone was an automatic ten years with five years pending, plus other outstanding felony charges, which were good for another ten to twenty years. And I loved the adrenaline rush of swerving through traffic. It was the same as pulling off an armed robbery.

Shenean kept looking over her shoulder, trying to decide when to drop the three hits of heroin out the window. I continued to glance in the rearview mirror at her. I wasn't sure if she was infatuated by the brigade of state police cars, or just hesitant to throw two hundred dollars of dope away. As much as she had a sweet tooth for heroin, I knew she would hold on to it until the last possible moment.

Dinky's eyes were glued to the road as we dodged in between an RV in the right lane and a Greyhound bus in the center. The RV lost control, swerving off the road. Dirt and dust swarmed around the vehicle like a cloud of smoke in an oil fire. Somehow, a Virginia State Police car traveling close to ninety or hundred, coming up in the right lane, was nipped by the RV, and went spinning in circles off the shoulder. Another trooper eased along my left side and I jolted in front, forcing him to hit the brakes. He went spinning across the median strip, boot-legging, ripping the grass up like a John Deere tractor.

I threw a smile in the rearview mirror, but Dinky never smiled, even when it looked like we were winning the race to Florida. She was petite with a small attractive face, spoke very softly with a strong Jamaican accent, and had the prettiest long fingernails I'd ever seen.

I had only known the girls for four or five hours, but I thought they would do well in Florida. With my gift of gab, I had always been comforting and soothing to strangers, and been able to read them very quickly. The girls liked the way I talked about all the money and the good times we were going to have in the Sunshine State.

Dinky cleared her throat as we shot past another bus and scurried around a tractor trailer in the right lane, "You crazy, Vinnie," she said with her sweet little accent.

"You like that?" I asked with a little humor. Her eyes jutted between the lanes, as we passed the fifty–five mile per hour traffic at mach speed. Cars appeared and disappeared within seconds. "We're going to be in Florida by midnight, girls. Look out! Here comes Vinny. Am I wheeling, Dinky? Am I the man?"

"Yeah," she whispered in a soft voice.

"Shenean," I said politely, leaning back over the seat, "you need to throw that dope out the window, girl. I'll buy you some more. I promise."

Taking a last hit of heroin, Shenean complained: "This ain't right, throwing good dope out the window. Something wrong with you, Vinnie. You're messed up. You ain't got no sense. You ain't suppose to waste stuff. I wouldn't have come if I'd had known this. Would I, Dinky? You tell him, sis. You know me."

Dinky never responded. She was too engrossed watching the state police cars, now numbering ten. The original unmarked state police car, which turned his lights on fifteen miles back at the Ladysmith exit, still cruised in the pack. Uniquely enough that exit would be the changing point of my life for eternity.

In the distance, two tractor trailers straddled the far left and right lanes, leaving the middle open. I slowed down to around eighty–five, approaching with caution, and decided to squeeze in between them. Easing quickly to within a hundred yards, I kicked the Buick for all she had, and climbed to hundred–fifteen, leaving the pack of state police cars in the distance, dodging traffic. I should have known, at that point, the two big rigs would be waiting for me.

A moment of nostalgia flashed in and out of my mind like an excerpt from a movie commercial. All I could see was my dad, mom, brother, and sisters. Who were they? They were like people I barely knew, casual acquaintances from the past. I was closer to my old cell mates than my own flesh and blood.

CHAPTER 2

I was the youngest of four children, born October 24, 1954, in a middle class home in East Baltimore. My father's ancestors were from Germany and my mother's from England. My father's father was a violent, hard, bitter man who arrived from Europe in the early 1900's. Occasionally, he beat his kids, his wife, and brawled with anyone who disagreed with him. He had a violent temper which was subject to going off at any moment. My father was a carbon copy of him.

Dad worked as a welder for the Washington Company in Baltimore and maintained a decent public image, being honored for work attendance and employee of the month. But at home, he was a different man; an alcoholic, a wife beater, a child abuser, and a man filled with rage and hate. He cursed with a passion and said he was a devout atheist, arguing and cursing the existence of a living God.

My earliest memories were of him coming home from work, breaking into a rage like a mad man because dinner wasn't ready, or somebody didn't say the right thing. He was unpredictable; anything could trigger his erratic behavior.

Derrick, being the oldest boy, was beaten much worst than the rest of us. Dad beat him with his fists, brooms, mops, rakes, and even once with a hammer. Sometimes the beatings were so bad, he wouldn't be able to attend school for a week. Dad physically threw him out of the house at age fourteen and Derrick went to live with my grandmother for awhile. Shortly thereafter, he was awarded to the state, spending several years in foster homes. At eighteen, he joined the army and was sent to Vietnam.

Sherry, the youngest girl, was the apple of dad's eye, getting by with much more than anyone else. That's not to say she didn't get her share of beatings, because she did. Sherry received top grades in high school, and eventually graduated from college.

Charlotte, the oldest girl, was a little more mischievous. She got her share of whippings, but they were not quite as violent as the beatings my brother and I endured. Eventually, Charlotte was sent to the Maryland Correctional Center for Juveniles for a year, and lived in a foster home for another two years.

Mom holding me, with
Dad looking on in front
of our house in Prince
George County

Dad and his dog in front of the house
in 1973. One of the few pictures of
him, as he refused to be photographed.

At age 6 in front of Dad's 1954 Chrysler

If dad got tired of hitting us with his strap, he'd resort to his hands and fists. It made him so mad that he couldn't make me cry, no matter how hard or how long he hit. Sometimes the pain was nearly unbearable, but I refused to break in front of him. Once, I was beaten so badly I could not walk. I crawled around like a paraplegic on the floor, and was out of school for two weeks. Nobody knows what perseverance we had to endure to stay alive.

The memory of being beaten-up Christmas morning and locked in my closet, with the dresser pulled in front of the door from early morning until late evening, still burns in my mind. Twelve long hours sitting in a dark closet without food or water was the ultimate torture for an eight year old boy. My stomach groaned and cried for food as the aroma of Christmas dinner seeped under the closet door from the kitchen. My mouth watered for the taste of dressing and gravy, even hours after the kitchen had been cleaned up and the dishes put away.

The only good memory I can recall was the Christmas of 1959, when I was five. I wanted a GI Joe in combat fatigues with the jeep and trailer. I remember sitting on Santa's lap telling him I wanted this more than anything in the world. Would he please, please, bring it to me? I had been a good boy.

In the backyard, we had an old '48 Plymouth which didn't run. It had been sitting there for years. I used to sit in the car for hours and pretend I was driving. I noticed something covered with a blanket in the back seat. I pulled the blanket up, and there were our Christmas presents, with my GI Joe, the jeep and trailer. I can't ever remember a happier day in my life! The only thing that bothered me was that my father was Santa. He wasn't the nice, jolly fat man with the white beard who visited our house once a year, but rather a violent hateful man, who lived in my house and beat me without reason.

Years later, driving over to his house to kill him, I thought about that
GI Joe the Christmas of 1959. It was the only nice thing I could remember he ever did for me.

                    *   *   *

My mother suffered from low self-esteem, which for the most part,
was a result of my father constantly belittling her. When she tried to
stop him from beating us, he would turn on her and beat her mercilessly. It was not unusual for her to have a black-eye, busted lip, and a
mass of bruises. Dad beat her so bad one night she fell to the floor
unconscious, leaving a puddle of blood in the hallway. He dragged her
by the hair into the bathroom, filled the tub with water and forced her
bloody face down into the water. Derrick tried to break his grip, but was
no match for dad, as the water turned pinkish. All of us were begging
and screaming, "Please, don't kill mom! Please, dad, don't."

He was like a man possessed by demons which gave him supernatural
strength. A frightening change came over him, with his eyes protruding
and his voice turning to a wretched tone. The purple blood vessels down
his neck appeared to be on the verge of popping. He lashed out with a
series of obscene words, desperately taking heavy breaths of air, before
finally letting mom go.

Sherry cried hysterically, while Charlotte comforted her. Derrick
attended to mom, getting her on her feet while she took large gulps of
air. Dad jolted out of the bathroom into the kitchen for a drink, still
cursing, and started beating on the refrigerator like it was one of us.

Minutes later, a police car stopped in front of the house, and I ran
out to greet them. "Please, don't take my daddy away," I cried as the two
officer opened the door of the patrol car. "Please don't."

"Calm down, son," the officer pleaded. "We need to talk to your dad."

One of the officers had been called to our house before, and was
familiar with the domestic problems and violence. He saw a heavy

bruise on my arm, and reached over with his hand to examine it closer. "How did you get the bruise, son?"

Catching me off guard, I wasn't sure what to say. Dad had beaten me the night before with his fist. I couldn't just tell the truth because I didn't want anyone to know. "Oh, playing baseball."

He seemed reluctantly satisfied, went inside, talked to dad and mom, wrote a report and left. Later, this information was used by social services to remove each of us from the home.

The whole event was forgotten after a few days. It was back to a daily environment of hate and violence from the moment dad arrived home until we were put to bed. There was never an expression of love, a kiss, a hug, or tenderness from him.

Christmas of 1963, Kenny Nickels, Derrick, and I broke into a neighbor's house, helping ourselves to the array of gifts from under their tree. We hauled the presents through the back door in broad daylight, and sat behind the garage opening them, while we sang Christmas carols. The family gave some of the crummiest gifts to each other for Christmas! The only thing we had any interest in was three–five pound boxes of candy. We sat there and gorged ourselves on fifteen pounds of chocolate candy before supper!

A few days later, we hit another neighbor's house and scored some decent stuff; a nice record player, five popular record albums, an expensive watch, and two silver bowls, which we re-wrapped for mom for Christmas. We unwrapped the presents this time before we hauled them away! I opened a box which had a pearl ring inside, and Kenny wanted to give it to a girl at school, which was fine with me. There was a twenty dollar bill on the dining room table which I stuffed in my pocket. I prowled around the house with a glass of milk and cookies looking for anything interesting. I found a pair of new leather gloves and matching hat in the back of a closet which had not been wrapped. I decided to give them to dad for Christmas.

We felt a sense of accomplishment as we left, having completed all our Christmas shopping at one place. We carried away a lot of items which we wrapped for Mom. She was surprised at the big Christmas. All she could do was smile, opening package after package. It never crossed my mind that dad might be wearing the stolen gloves and hat in front of the neighbors one day.

*   *   *

Mom did everything possible to keep the family together, taking all the kids to church on Sunday. She tried to make up for what was lacking in our home. She was a devoted mother and wife, who didn't want to leave her husband, but finally, after a severe beating, she packed our clothes and left. What a difficult decision, being on her own with four children and no job.

We stayed at my grandmother's house for two months. At first, we felt relief and safety. Derrick seemed the most relieved, because for some reason dad hated him more than anyone. The girls were quite happy also, getting away from the violence and hatred. Dad begged mom to return home. He promised he would change, would never harm us again, and would be the father and husband she wanted him to be. In a moment of weakness, she returned, but he never kept any of his promises.

*   *   *

Kenny Nickels and I continued to break in houses after the Christmas season. It became a sport, just something to do. We slashed tires, dropped bricks off bridges onto cars, threw coke bottles at houses, and beat up kids. I took my father's rifle and shot at a few people for fun, with no intent to hurt or kill. Kenny and I would break into one neighbor's basement periodically and steal his wine he had stored. Both of us would get drunk and sick, wondering why anyone wanted to drink the stuff. However, we continued breaking in and gulping down the purple juice on a weekly basis.

Both of us liked to fight. After we became more experienced in drinking, our aggressive, violent, nature increased. We roamed the neighborhood looking for action. Whether it was older boys or someone coming into our territory, we would strike out at them. Hate and violence were like a poison we enjoyed. Watching others being afraid of us became intoxicating.

I got sick to think it, but I was becoming a hateful-violent person just like my father.

*   *   *

A large department store opened about a mile from my house. People were mobbing the place with the grand opening sales. Kenny and I walked up to the store to see what was happening. In the parking lot, a local DJ was pumping the crowd with free records and tee shirts. Inside, the store was a mad house with people shopping like it was Christmas Eve. We strolled through with a shopping cart, picking up a couple of store bags at the door. We stood by the checkout counter waiting for a person carrying a large item to their car who needed help. We finally grabbed an elderly couple, told them we were trying to win a good citizen's award by helping seniors with their bags. They simply loved us. It gave them hope for the new generation. We put our bags with their bags in the shopping cart and walked out past the guard at the door, appearing to be the grandchildren. It was almost too easy.

The stealing became habit forming. It was that rush of accomplishment and superiority over those in authority. During the grand opening sale, we made three trips to the store for merchandise each day. We'd sell the goods, come up with a nice wad of money, and go to the pool hall.

At twelve, I had become a skilled thief and intimidator (not only of kids my age, but kids of fifteen and sixteen). I wasn't particularly big, but extremely aggressive, challenging anyone to a fight. I couldn't wait for someone to say the wrong words to me, because I had so much hate and anger built up inside. In the seventh grade, getting into fights was a daily event with me. I loved it, and everyone knew it. If there had been honors for the seventh grade class, I would have been voted "most likely to end up in prison." Word of my violent nature spread quickly to all of my teachers, except possibly my math teacher.

He made a remark about me in class which was embarrassing. Within seconds, I was out of control. I picked up a chair and threw it, hitting him in the head. Charging like a raging bull, I began throwing punches in a flurry, pounding him in the face. He fought back, crushing me against the wall with his two hundred pound body. I punched and kicked harder, connecting with several solid blows. I was going mad, in my own zone of violence, just like dad. The girls screamed, some of the boys went for help. Someone yelled, "Darron, stop it! Stop it!"

I couldn't stop. With others helping, the teacher had me on the floor with my hands pinned, two other kids held my feet, and all I could do was head butt and bite. The principal and two other teachers ran into the room, trying to restore order. They held me on the floor until I calmed down. I could feel the violence and hate…this super adrenaline, slowly leaving my body.

The cops arrived and took me downtown in a police car. I thought it was cool that the kids in my class were able to see me handcuffed and put in the back seat of a patrol car. It was a merit badge in crime, which I relished so badly. This became my first charge of assault and battery.

My parents came to the police precinct three hours later and retrieved me. I dreaded the drive home. No sooner than I entered the door, my father tore into me, doing something which the math teacher couldn't. He beat me with a strap, and then slapped me around until his hand was bloody. I remained defiant, refusing him the pleasure of seeing me cry. This only made him more angry, but gave me more reasons to want to kill him.

Suspended from school, awaiting charges before a juvenile judge, I used my days wisely, going back to the department store for more goods. After the grand opening sale, the store wasn't as crowded and it became more difficult to steal. Kenny and I devised a new plan.

"Look," I told him, "Let's get fifty or seventy–five dollars worth of stuff, have Bobby Byrd meet us inside, and take it to the customer service line in a bag."

Kenny called Bobby Byrd "Deadwood" because he was mentally handicapped, and always wanted to hang out with us. He was eighteen, but looked twenty–one. Bobby was easily intimidated by Kenny who was only fourteen.

"No receipt, man," Kenny shot back.

"People return stuff all the time without receipts," I told him.

"What's Deadwood going to get for his troubles?" Kenny questioned, lighting up a cigarette.

"Twenty–five, and we'll let him hang out with us for a day."

"Let's do a hundred dollars of clothes, and make it worth it," Kenny said, exhaling a long stream of smoke through his nose.

"How about a man's suit or an overcoat?"

"Sure. That oughta run about a hundred."

The plan worked so well, we decided to try it again the next day with different people at the counter. Another home run, until we got outside and I got caught stealing a silk shirt. Security started asking Deadwood questions, and he sang like a canary in a concert hall. "Kenny and Darron came up with the idea. They were going to give me twenty–five dollars every time I went through the line."

I felt proud adding another merit badge to my crime sheet, my first shoplifting charge. My parents picked me up at the police precinct. Dad gave me that cold, steely-eyed stare which meant he was going to teach me a lesson. As soon as we arrived home, he beat me with the strap and with his fist like an alley fighter in a brawl. The sound of his fist hitting my flesh echoed loudly through the house. From the living room, mother begged him to stop numerous times, but she stayed clear of the bedroom. Dad continued pounding away like he was the hometown champion fighting for the title, and I was the smart-mouthed hoodlum who wanted his belt. I fought hard but was no match for a five–eleven, two hundred–fifty pound brawler. My only victory was he couldn't make me cry, no matter how hard or how many times he hit. It made me think, falsely, that maybe I had won.

Within a week, I was caught shoplifting again. This time on April 14, 1966, I was put in a holding and processing unit at a detention center called Waxsters. It was a place I returned to again, again, and again.

Waxsters Juvenile Center, the receiving and processing center,
where I was sent at age 12.

Chapter 3

Handcuffed, sitting in the back seat of a sheriff's car, we entered the complex known as Waxsters. The juvenile judge, after the social services report on the home environment and the presentation of charges, awarded me to the state for an indefinite period. He felt it best that I be awarded to the state to be raised in the system with state programs than stay in my home. Mother cried at the hearing, watching her youngest son taken away in handcuffs. Dad was unemotional, not saying anything during the hearing to help me. He seemed relieved of a burden and responsibility he probably never wanted.

My response, as the car pulled in behind the two–twelve foot high fences, was not fear, but more anger. I was furious with my parents, the judge, social services, and the system. I hated my father for bringing me into the world.

I looked over the area as a new tenant, wondering what the place had in store for me. It was a fairly new building with heavy, steel-slotted screens on every window and secured steel doors. It was not only the receiving and processing unit for juvenile offenders, but a holding unit for boys from Baltimore and Prince George County. Whoever did the diagnostic evaluation must have been aware of a territorial division between the boys in the two counties, because it was always about even in every building, fifteen from each area. Most of the guys were fourteen, fifteen, and sixteen years old. I was only twelve at the time, and smaller than most of the them.

I was determined not to be intimidated when I arrived in the unit. Within a short period, you had to prove yourself that you weren't a punk. Someone would always test you.

In 1966, juveniles could smoke in the day room of the detention center. I had only been there a short time when I asked the guy next to me for an ashtray. He said something smart, and that did it. I tore into him, knocking him and his chair to the floor. The guards broke up the fight, and threw both of us into the lock-down cells. Later, Chick Reese and I became good friends. We spent years together in the juvenile system, and eventually spent adult time in both Hagerstown New Jail and Jessup Correctional Center.

The lock-down unit was six feet by eight feet with a single two inch mat on the floor, and no outside windows. The thick, three inch steel door had a single lock and a small rectangular six–by–six inch glass window. I thought for sure I could get out somehow, so I kicked and rammed the door for about a half day, until I finally gave up. Chick across the hall, yelled, "You'll break your shoulder before you break the door."

We had nothing better to do than become friends.

"How long have you been here?" I asked Chick through the door.

"Two weeks."

"Have you thought of any way to get out?"

"It's been on my mind since the day I got here. But we need to be in a better place than the lock-down cells to have a chance."

"Like where," I asked.

"Like the place we were when you started the fight with me." Chick said bitterly as he shouted through the crack in the doorway. "I was planning on leaving the next day until you screwed it up."

"Look, I'm sorry. You should've been more polite when I asked for the ashtray."

"Nobody's polite around here."

"Who's going with you?"

"A couple of the guys who were sitting next to me in the dayroom."

"Cut me in."

"I'll think about it."

A week later, out of lock-down, we had yard time. Chick, another guy and I made a run for the twelve foot fence which had no razor wire. Scaling over the first fence quite easily, we make a mad dash to the second fence, climbing like wild monkeys to the top, to the cheers of our colleagues in the yard. No sooner had we landed on the other side than the guards were waiting, bull-riding us to the ground. We were shackled, cuffed, and taken back inside for two weeks of lock-down.

This second time in lock-down slowly crept by at a snails pace. The little freedom of being joined again with the rest of the unit was one small spot of joy. Almost immediately, Chick Reese and I started plotting another escape, which we were never able to carry out at Waxsters.

The boys I met in Waxsters…Chick Reese, Dewy Bell, Albert "Pineapple" Jackson, Joe Mondelli, Baby Ug Mug (an ugly kid whose last name was Mug), Freddy Cousins, Snoop (never knew his real name) Johnson, Mike Mizell, and Jerry "Bee" Coleman stayed with me all six years through the juvenile system. After Waxsters, we continually met each other at different units and were cell mates at times. Strangely enough, seven years later, we found ourselves sitting at the same table in the dining hall of the New Jail in Hagerstown, serving adult time.

*   *   *

After thirty days in Waxsters (twenty–one days in lock-down), I was sent to the Maryland Children Center for further evaluation. I was assigned a counselor by the name of Miss White, an attractive, twenty–five year old lady, who seemed genuinely concerned about me.

Not only did I have a teenage crush on her, but I tried to be an exceptional student for the first time in my life. I wanted her to like me, and I knew my fate in the juvenile system rested in her hands.

An inmate by the name of James Cruger made a sly remark about Miss White having a big nose. Instantly, I took offense and jumped on Cruger. I beat him like a wild barbarian boxer against a New York account. I clobbered away like a punching machine, hammering him to the floor, until the unit staff pulled me off and took me back to lock-down. As a teenager, it was my finest hour of southern chivalry.

Days later, Miss White wanted to know what started the fight, so I told her: "Cruger said you have a big nose."

"I think it was gallant of you, and I appreciate you wanting to protect my honor," she said, "but it was not necessary."

"Well, I thought it was necessary."

"Just because someone says something you don't agree with, you don't have to physically harm him."

"Miss White, maybe you don't have to take a stand, but I'm not backing down from anybody that says something I don't like."

The upper photo is the cottages where we were housed and the grounds of the Maryland Training Center for Boys. The lower photo is the entrance to the facility.

"Sooner or later, you'll learn differently," she said as she wrote a short paragraph in my personal folder.

I was convinced Miss White would be lenient in her evaluation of me because of the circumstances. Boy, was I wrong! She recommended incarceration in the Maryland Training School for Boys for an indefinite time with special treatment classes for those with violent natures.

*   *   *

The first day at the Maryland Training School for Boys, I walked out of my building to see six guys beating one boy in the corner. I remember the long, stringy, blond hair the kid had, and how relentless the six boys were beating him. I watched with several others, knowing this violent system was survival. Miss White was well-educated, but didn't know anything about survival, which was always marked by violence. She would have been like the blond hair boy, beaten to the ground and left for dead.

My mom came weekly for Saturday visitation. She brought a special treat, McDonald's cheeseburgers, fries, and a Coke. It was her way of making up for the dysfunctional family, and all the suffering we had endured. She seemed so hurt having to see her youngest son incarcerated in a juvenile prison, a ward of the state of Maryland. Her eyes were always on the brink of tears, with pain and disappointment, especially when we had to say good-bye. She would choke, turn away quickly, and never look back. I knew she was crying all the way back to the car. I'd press my head against the bars until she was out of sight, knowing it would be seven more days before I'd see my mom again.

One Saturday she brought my sister Sherry, but because of her age she was not allowed inside to see me. She stood outside the building by the window of my cell calling, "Brother, can you hear me?" She would pause, and call again, "Are you in there, Darron? It's me, Sis."

I heard every word, but I didn't want her to see me through the bars. Humiliated? Disgraced? I don't know. Probably.

She would not leave. "It's Sis. Are you in there?"

Finally, after I knew she wouldn't leave, I went to the window, pressing my head against the bars, looking out. Sherry looked liked Shirley Temple with her hair in a ponytail, lipstick, and makeup on, and all dressed up.

"Mom said this window was your room. Did you just wake up?" Her eyes filled with tears as she looked up at her baby brother.

"Yeah, Sherry, I just woke up," I said, trying to hold back the emotions in my voice. If anyone could make me cry, it would be Sherry. She was so innocent and childlike standing by my window. I thought of how she faithfully fixed me breakfast before I went to school, helping mama take care of the kids.

"Will you be home for Christmas?"

I may never see another Christmas at home, I thought, after reading Miss White's evaluation...indefinite term recommended. Painfully, I replied, "No, I won't be home this Christmas."

"Maybe right after Christmas?"

"Yeah, right after Christmas." My heart ached to tell her it would be a long time before I got out.

"I bought you a present. I'll save it for you."

My head pressed against the bars as I watched her walk to the car, finally fading out of sight. It would be eight years before I'd see her again, until I escaped from the Brockridge Correctional Center.

*   *   *

Mr. McKenean was the cottage supervisor for my unit at the Maryland Training School for Boys. For some reason, he never liked me. On numerous occasions, he let that be known. The unit had a long hallway with fifteen rooms on each side. Each room had a steel door which was locked after seven o'clock.

One evening, my door was left unlocked. Mr. McKenean told Dewy Bell to go into my room after lights were out and beat me. (Dewy told me this years later while we were serving time at Hagerstown Prison). I was not a sound sleeper, so as soon as the door squeaked open, I awakened. Dewy charged toward me. I reached under my pillow for my ink pen, and stabbed the dark in a wild rage, finally striking flesh. I kept jamming toward the scream. Feeling something warm and mushy on my hands, I knew I had drawn blood. On my feet, I kept moving toward the body that retreated to the doorway, cursing and challenging it. He finally went running down the hallway to his cell, leaving a trail of blood drops which I followed the next morning to Dewy Bell's cell. Dewy was mysteriously missing, sent to another unit. Mr. McKenean never said anything to me after the incident.

A week later, I was on my way with five other boys to Hagerstown, Maryland to a group home run by the Mennonites. I liked the home-made food. The people were nice, but a little too religious for me. Unfortunately, I had a problem getting along with the boys. I was entering the turf of a group of twelve guys, who had lived there for awhile. Immediately I was challenged, and ended up having to fight ten out of the twelve.

After a week, the six of us left the home at midnight, walked over to Route 40, and started hitchhiking. It was ridiculous, but all six of us stood on the side of the road together trying to catch a ride. One of the guys remarked, "Nobody's going to pickup six hitchhikers." Someone else replied, "Maybe some idiot will come along with a bus and give us a ride." Sure enough, about fifteen minutes later, two hippies came along in a 58 Ford Country Squire station wagon with hand painted flowers and peace signs all over it. All six of us piled in and rode back to Baltimore. By three o'clock the next day, the police had arrested all of us for loitering. Once again, we were on our way back to Waxsters.

I spent the next six months uneventfully, at the Maryland Training School for Boys. I went for a yearly review before the board, never expecting the possibility of a discharge after the last escape from the foster home. When I was released before my fourteenth birthday and sent home, I was stunned.

Sherry now lived in Baltimore; Charlotte resided in a group home in Prince George County; and Derrick stayed in a foster home north of Baltimore. From the first day back home, I knew my father didn't want me there. It would have been better if I had not been released. His hatred for Derrick was passed on to me. I was the only one left.

Being back on the streets was great; no more fences, no lock-down cells, and freedom at last. Almost two years of my life had been wasted behind fences, and now I wanted to live. I hooked up with Kenny Nickels and his friends who had a nice gig breaking into houses, stealing cars, selling marijuana and pills. I liked the scene. They were "my kind of guys".

We ventured out as young entrepreneurs. A low income housing development had opened down the street and became prime territory for our new portfolio of products.

I registered for school and was placed in the eighth grade. It was exciting to be in a real school, around girls and all the high school activities. The first home football game and first dance of the year were coming up in three weeks. I thought, "I've arrived just in time."

At the end of my second week, my social studies teacher, Mr. Albertson, said something to me about my shirt tail being out as I was leaving the school grounds. I turned and gave him an obscene gesture. He said, "I'll see you tomorrow, Mr. Shipe."

I came into class late the next day. He stopped teaching and said, "Mr. Shipe, I'll see you after class. You need to be taught some manners and I'm the one to teach you."

Everyone was looking at me, wondering what I had done. I stood to my feet, calmly walked up to him, and slapped him in the face as hard as I could. He charged toward me, and I unleashed a series of punches, hitting him in the face and head. Some of the boys held me back, and dragged me into the hallway.

That was my last day inside a public school in the state of Maryland. I was only one week away from going to my first dance.

The police arrived about a half hour later, and carried me off.

CHAPTER 4

Handcuffed in the back seat of a sheriff's car, I returned to Waxsters. My new born freedom had lasted a total of thirteen days. My counselor suggested I apparently couldn't make it on the outside. Doubts sprouted in my mind about the same thing. My spirit dropped as a sense of desperation consumed me. I never thought in my wildest dreams that incarceration would be my destiny in life. Regrets of not being able to control my temper and adapt to society haunted me. Was I going to have to resign myself to this type of life forever? Not only did I hate myself, but I also hated everyone else.

From Waxsters, I was sent back to the Maryland Training School for Boys, where it was the same old routine of fighting, and disciplinary action. I was placed in the senior section for boys fifteen through seventeen, although I was only fourteen. One reason I was always fighting was because I was small, and I felt I had to prove myself. I walked around with a chip on my shoulder, waiting to lash out at anyone.

Through a strange recommendation, Joe Mondelli, Mike Mizell, and I were on a list to be sent to a Forestry Camp in the mountains of Garrett County. At first, we though it was an honor being selected, but it was sheer punishment.

The three of us rode in a van to a small town called Piedmont, Maryland at the base of the Savage River State Forest. Piedmont holds the distinction of being the worst smelling town in North America, due

to the foul odor of the pulp mill. The general store had a meager selec-
tion of supplies…one can of each brand of soup, a couple cans of tuna
fish, a box of Quaker Oats, and a can of Spaghetti-O's! We stood around
making jokes about Piedmont while waiting for our ride. We were shuttled up the mountain to a loggers work camp for juvenile offenders. It
was a brutal place, desolate and isolated, far away from civilization, but
no fences.

A brawny logger whose arms were bigger than our legs met us. He
was right down nasty looking with hair growing on his chest thicker
than a brown grizzly bear's. He taunted us from the first day with,
"There'll always be a place here for you. We'll have a bed waiting." He
clearly could read our mind set, knowing we were planning our escape
from the moment we arrived.

Some of the boys at the camp were seventeen and eighteen years old.
We didn't fit in with them at all. We concluded they were working on
their college degrees in forestry, so they kept to themselves. They were
seniors, receiving the special privileges of easy jobs with the higher pay
of 90 cent a day. Our starting pay was 30 cent a day; a $1.50 a week.

Every Friday, they loaded us on a Department of Correction's bus
and drove us to the store for candy. Sounds trivial, but it was a special
treat. They allowed two boys to leave the bus at a time to go inside. This
way, they could keep an eye on us. Otherwise, we'd have robbed the
store blind, like a bunch of small termites eating soft wood. But even
then, we managed to steal a few items when one of us would ask the
officer a question, allowing the other to palm a candy bar in his coat.

Joe, Mike, and I decided we were going to take a leave of absence after
the first week. After bed check, we slipped out the window. Instead of
taking the main road which we knew was watched, we took the railroad
tracks down the mountainside. It was one of the worst decisions we ever
made. Six hours later, after walking all night, we finally made it to the
bottom. Exhausted and hungry, we found an empty boxcar in the rail
yard and slept for two hours until we heard the sounds of people from

the camp looking for us. We made a dash for the woods with the camp guards and the seniors in hot pursuit. I dove into the river and started floating downstream, hoping to escape to the other side. The current was brisk, but a senior out swam the current and dragged me ashore.

After returning to the camp, we were put on disciplinary duty. The big, brutish guard said, "I told you boys there would always be a place here for you." He had his own agenda set for us. Our first task was to dig up stumps; the hardest possible job at camp. To remove one stump, it would take nearly a half day digging and axing the roots loose from the hard clay soil. It was rough physical work from six in the morning until five o'clock in the evening.

After a tree had been brought down, we had to trim the branches and limbs. Next, we had a two-man cross blade saw to cut the tree into logs. One by one, we hauled the heavy logs to a pile for loading.

Our greatest concern were the rattlesnakes which hid in the fallen limbs and piles of heavy brush on the ground. There was never a day we didn't see at least one snake.

One afternoon, I was walking nonchalantly to the water cooler, stepping over a log with small brush around it. As my foot came down in the brush, a rattlesnake was coiled and ready to strike. My foot was in mid air, and I couldn't move in another direction as I heard the rattlers. The snake lunged with lightning speed, striking my boots. Strangely, his fang hung in my boot with his mouth wide open. The snake shook wildly, trying to break loose, coiling and recoiling rapidly.

I hollered for my brawny logger friend, who rushed over with a gritty grin on his face. He stepped on the snake's tail, then took his hunting knife and sliced the rattlesnake in half with one whack. Half the snake cringed on the ground recoiling in circles, while the other half hung to my boot. He cut the head loose from my boot and the snake fell to the ground. "All right boy, get back to work. You're all right," he uttered without the slightest concern for my well being.

Six months dragged by until we finished the program, then it was back to the Maryland Training Center for Boys. I was put into a unit with Snoop Johnson, Freddy Cousins, and Albert "Pineapple" Jackson. Snoop had the longest nose of any human who has ever walked this earth. It dangled from his face like a small elephant's trunk. For four years, I never heard anyone call him by his real first name. Freddy Cousins was a street thug and thief from downtown Baltimore. He would steal anything from an extra slice of bread in the chow line, to a name badge off a guard. He had a trophy box full of badges. Albert "Pineapple" Jackson, a cool Hawaiian dude, became a good friend over the years. He had a wild outrageous hairdo that was coned like the top of a pineapple. He was in for stealing cars. I joked with him, "You should have told the judge you didn't speak English, let your attorney call you a foreign exchange student, and claimed diplomatic immunity!"

We spent a lot of private time talking about our families, our dreams, and what we were going to do when we were released from the system. Sadly, none of our dreams ever came true. Years later, we all ended up incarcerated in the same place, still talking about the same old dreams in the adult system.

*   *   *

Buddy Davis, Pineapple Jackson, Freddy Cousins, and I were given another opportunity by my probation officer, Tracy Stalworth. He suggested we be sent to West Palm Beach Military Academy in Florida, which sounded great to us! Actually, we were given an alternative, either serve time in the Maryland Training School for Boys, or the military program in Florida. The counselors thought military training would teach us discipline. We jumped at the chance of going to Florida.

Pineapple and I went back to our units to prepare to leave. "Hey, Pineapple, they're goin' to make you cut your hair," I told him as we gathered up our few worldly belongings.

"Man, I'm not cutting my hair," Pineapple said seriously. "I ain't doin' any marching, either. I don't like marching."

"You know they're going to make a soldier out of you."

"The only thing I like about Florida is the hot weather and girls on the beach."

"I can see you now in your uniform," I joked, "chasing girls on the beach. You'll be looking like an Hawaiian king's son."

"You don't know what you're in for, man."

Pineapple was so right. None of us knew what we were in for; nor did they.

Two guards took us to the Baltimore-Washington Airport, where we caught a Piedmont Airline flight. Upon arriving in West Palm, a military officer drove us to the academy, which was like a miniature West Point with boys in a field marching and drilling. Some were exercising, others were standing at attention like stone statues with grumpy, old men shouting in their faces.

Within two hours, we had gotten haircuts, and were issued clothing, bed linens, and dormitory assignments. A sixteen year old sergeant accompanied us through the basic institution's military information; how to carry ourselves as boys of the West Palm Beach Military Academy and the military code of justice, which we were to memorize. We anxiously awaited the end of the first day to see if they were going to draft us as reinforcements for the South Vietnam conflict. They made us feel like the world's security depended upon our being militarily prepared, and combat ready.

It was rather exciting for the first two months. I truly made a sincere effort to do well and the Colonel noticed I had potential leadership qualities. He promoted me to sergeant, where I was given special privileges, the best details, and leave time.

But in all honesty, this was not my cup of tea. During the second month, Buddy Davis and I walked out the front door and left. There was no security and no fences, only a bed check at ten o'clock. We walked two miles to a housing development, stole a new El Camino, and drove to town. We were looking good, cruising the streets of West Palm, talking to girls, and hanging out at a video arcade until midnight. Everyone thought we were a couple of rich kids with the new car, but the truth was we didn't even have twenty–five cents to buy a Coke.

"Where did you get the car?" one of the girls asked.

"I got it for my sixteenth birthday," Buddy said.

Another girl observed, "That's a nice car. How come the side window's broken out?"

"Somebody tried to break into it at school," I said. "You can't have anything nice these days that somebody won't try to tear up." I was hoping she didn't notice the steering column which I had partially ripped to pieces with a screwdriver to hot wire.

We slipped into our dormitory at two–thirty after dropping off the car. First call was five–thirty and we struggled to make revelry formation at six. We were dead tired. Nevertheless, we went along with the program. It was a typical busy day, learning how to march, assembling and re-assembling rifles, and studying military code.

In the third month, Pineapple, Buddy, Freddy and I started breaking into lockers, stealing anything of value…radios, cassettes, jewelry and money. We shuttled the goods to a street fence, someone had told us about, and turned it to cash.

The mail arrived at ten–thirty and was sorted. The room stayed locked until five when they had mail call. So at noon, Pineapple and I broke into the mailroom, opened the packages and sifted through the letters for money. We picked up twenty or thirty dollars, lots of cookies, a few pieces of jewelry, cameras, and plenty of photographs.

A short time later, Freddy and Buddy beat up an underclassman who caught them breaking into his locker. They were assigned to a discipline class, and given a weeks KP duty which worked out quite well. When the meats and canned supplies arrived for the week, we helped ourselves to the goods and sold them to the fence.

Several times a week we'd sneak into town to see the girls, until we got caught one evening by an officer. That was pretty well it for me. Everything was mounting up as another failure in life. I couldn't tell if it was a syndrome or a strange hand of fate sending me down the road to destruction. Nothing in my life was turning out good. Apparently, I had the heart of a criminal; there was no changing me.

The third strike against me happened in a confrontation with a lieutenant. I grabbed a baseball bat, hit him on the head, and beat him badly. They transported him to the hospital, bleeding, and unconscious.

Midway through the fourth month, all of us from Baltimore were dismissed from the program. We flew back home, wondering where we would end up next.

*   *   *

Tracy Stalworth was a cool guy, who was genuinely concerned about me. Although he had to abide by the rules of being my probation officer, he would do extra things for me, like buying me lunch, taking me over to his apartment, and buying small personal items which I needed.

Tracy received a letter from the Juvenile Justice System requesting that I be sent home. My dad made known his disappointment and personal dislike for me starting that first day. I was hiding under my bed when he picked up the phone and called Tracy. Mother begged him not to call, but nothing was going to stop him.

"Mr. Stalworth, this is Mr. Shipe, Darron's father. I don't want him back here. You got that. He can't stay in my house." He paused momentarily as if to listen to Stalworth. "The boy is trouble, just no good. Now, you find another place for him. Do you hear me?" Dad's voice was loud and angry.

Tracy replied with something which obviously made Dad mad. "Let me tell you something, Stalworth. If you don't get Darron out of my house, I'm going to throw him out real quick. Do you understand me?

I'll give you three days to find a place for him," he screamed at the top of his lungs, slamming the phone down, cursing the day I was born.

I laid under the bed, wanting to cry, because nobody wanted me. Only fifteen years old, I didn't know where I was going to lay my head that night. I locked my jaw tight so I wouldn't cry, and thought: Why doesn't someone want me? All I want is to be loved and noticed like a normal kid. My own father hates me and doesn't want me.

Right then, my heart hardened with a bitterness towards dad which I thought I'd never be able to relinquish. The very thought of killing him brought comfort to my mind, because he was the blame for our family's problems.

*   *   *

Three days later, Tracy picked me up and we drove to a group home in downtown Baltimore. There were twenty boys in the home. From the initial greeting, I knew my stay was limited. Only hours after arriving I was in a fight with one of the guys, mainly, because I had so much anger and bitterness in my life that I needed to take it out on someone. I was branded as a troublemaker. Quite honestly, I earned my title the next couple of months with an array of fights and a stealing binge. I was asked to leave and, once again, I was out on the streets with nowhere to go.

Tracy picked me up, stuffed my two bags of clothes into his trunk, and drove to Mr. and Mrs. Zingelmann's. They had a foster home which was registered with the state of Maryland in the East Riverdale section of Prince George County. They had ten boys in their home, and a special gift of making everyone feel important and a part of the family. Everyone respected the Zingelmanns. From the first day, I saw something special in them. They really cared. Not only were they strict, but they were fair, demanding that everyone attend church on Sundays and Wednesdays. Evidently, there was a state statute which said they couldn't teach or indoctrinate us on religion in the home, but there was no law which said they couldn't take us to church.

At age 15, in front of a group home in downtown West Baltimore. I was dismissed after thirty days for fighting and theft.

Their church was lively, with everyone singing their hearts out, and a few of the ladies dancing around with the joy of the Lord. We all thought it was pretty strange.

I ended up doing my usual thing, ravaging through the house, stealing anything of value. After starting several fights, I was asked to leave by the Zingelmanns after only six months. It pained them greatly, but there was no other choice in the matter.

Thoroughly disappointed, Tracy met me at the front door, helping me with my two bags of clothes to the car. He drove me to the home of Mr. and Mrs. Browning, a foster family in Prince George County, less than two miles from the Zingelmanns.

The Browning's had eight boys in their home. I lasted four months. One morning in February, the next door neighbor was warming up his new white Chrysler Imperial while he was in the house. I could almost hear the Imperial singing, "Take me for a drive." In a weak moment, I hurtled the hedge between the houses, jumped behind the wheel, and drove off.

I brought it back an hour later, but it didn't seem to make much difference to anyone. My fate was again sealed. The Prince George County police filed a report because it was a criminal offense, but they did not process it because the neighbors did not file charges.

Tracy picked me up, and scolded me about how poor my decision-making was. He was angrier than I had ever seen him: "Darron, you don't think, son. You knew the Brownings would ask you to leave after such a stunt. They offered you a nice home. You put me in a bad position trying to find a place for you at the last minute."

"You can do it, Tracy," I said trying to encourage him. "Hey, look, I'm sorry about the Brownings. I've apologize to them and the next door neighbor." I watched him shake his head in disgust, and I knew how personal he took everything.

"We're running out of places for you," Tracy pleaded with a loud voice.

"Maybe I could stay with you for a few days," I said.

He didn't see the humor or seriousness of my statement. Tracy could never envision me staying with him. He made several phone calls, desperately trying to find a place. Hours later, he found another foster home. Mr. and Mrs. Holgrim accepted me temporarily, until the paperwork from the state could be completed. By the time the paperwork was done, the Holgrims had asked me to leave because I had threatened a neighbor.

For days Tracy looked for a new foster home, until he ran across a new state program, Youth Development Center on the fifth floor of the YMCA in downtown Baltimore. In this half-way house for juveniles, I had my own room overlooking four lanes of Franklin Street with a Swedish Massage Parlor sign flashing in my window all night. The conditions of the program were that you had to pay rent and have a job. The staff monitored the building, and your presence for bed check, by eleven.

I felt like I could make it in this program. For once, a high level of optimism filled my mind. I was on my own and had a chance to prove I could make it. I thought about dropping Tracy Stalworth a thank you note for all the help he had offered, but I never did. I got my first job down the street as a dishwasher in the evenings. Unfortunately, it lasted only two weeks before I was caught stealing.

I walked a block down the street and was hired as a dishwasher in another small restaurant. This job lasted less than a week. It was the same story. Again, I got caught for stealing.

Across the street was the Swedish Massage Parlor, so I thought I would try for a job. Just what type of opening they had really didn't matter. I needed to eat and make rent each week. There were three girls sitting in the foyer, making humorous comments as I asked for the manager.

"She's out for lunch, honey, and won't be back for awhile," one of the girls said with a large smile. "What can we do for you?"

"I want to see the manager for a job."

"A job?" an attractive blond sitting on the sofa asked. All the other girls laughed at my naive youthfulness.

"He wants a job!" another girl shouted with an even bigger laugh. "How old are you?"

"Almost seventeen."

"In other words, sixteen. You're contributing to the delinquency of a minor, Trishia," the girl standing said. ·

"I'm not contributing to anything," she snapped back.

Finally I caught the thrust of what was going on and became slightly embarrassed. I told them, "I'm in the Youth Development Center Program. Do any of you know where I can get a good job?"

They threw back blank looks as if they didn't know what a good job was.

"What's your name?" the girl standing asked sincerely.

"Darron."

"Look, Darron, do you know where Center Street is?"

"Yeah."

"There is a little hamburger place called Buttery. How about going there and getting us lunch. We'll give you a few dollars."

"Sure."

The girls gathered at the counter to put in their orders, and I raced around the corner for burgers and fries. The girls gave me a ten dollar tip. I was ecstatic because I was only making a $1.75 an hour washing dishes. I liked this job! There was no question in my mind where I was going the next day.

In fact, I arrived at ten–thirty to make sure I was on time my first day. I didn't want the girls to think I wasn't dependable. As soon as I arrived, Trishia, the girl who did most of the talking the day before, caught me at the door. "Hey Darron, run over to Field's Drugs and get me a pair of black fishnet panty hose. Petite size. Here's five dollars, Sweety."

I didn't show the least bit of reluctance, because I wanted to be as efficient as possible with good service. This was one job where I didn't want to get fired.

"Hey honey," another called, "get me and Candy two bagels and cream cheese at the deli."

*   *   *

I arrived every morning at ten–thirty and ran errands for the girls. The rest of the day I hung out in the lobby, talking with them. They treated me like a little brother. It seemed like family, something I'd never experienced, with people really caring about me. All together there were six girls, Trisha, Candy, Bonnie, Marsha, Geneva, and Juanita. I don't know why, but Geneva and Juanita seemed to like me the best. On my birthday, they gave me a silk shirt and bought me lunch, which was the most recognition I could ever remember on my birthday. At Christmas, the girls got together and gave me a silk suit.

Everytime I wore the suit, I thought of the girls. Years later, it saddened me to think back on how hard the streets were on these people. Trisha, at age 26, was shot and killed by a jealous lesbian lover. Bonnie, age 25, was in a psychiatric hospital in Baltimore because of drug addiction. The other girls were either on heroin, speed, or alcohol and had faded away in six months to a year, never to be heard from again.

It was a high price to pay for living on the streets of Baltimore. Trying to survive was the only game in town, and the casualties were high.

Around the corner, there was a place called The Block with virtually door to door night clubs on both sides of the street. This area was the Mecca of street activity, with people walking from one bar to the next, all hours of the night. Drugs, prostitution, stolen property, and weapons were sold openly with little discretion. All the action intrigued me. I carried calling cards from the girls at the Swedish Massage Parlor, staying alert to anyone looking for a good time. I passed them out as if the massage parlor was giving free milk baths to desert travelers. Almost immediately, I started getting results. The next morning, the girls gave me fifty dollars and I was in business.

My good fortune and the turn of events in my life overwhelmed me. Nothing good had ever happened to me before. I spent my new wealth on clothes. I made fifty to sixty dollars in a single day, which was almost more than I earned as a dishwasher for a full week. Soon, I was the best dressed guy in YDC with everyone complimenting me on how well I was doing, and how nice my clothes looked. It made me feel good. I started walking with a little swagger in my step, probably just to show off my new pair of fifty–five dollar Italian leather Tony Borona shoes.

My next door neighbor at YDC was a black kid named Kenny Harris. "Hey, man, where'd you get that clean set of threads?" He jokingly asked, all the time eyeing me up and down with envy.

"Working, man, I don't play. I got to look good." I told him.

"Dishwashers must get paid good, where you're at!"

"Decent."

"Do you want to go in on some juice, and get jacked-up?"

Kenny was known as the juice man, because he'd been shooting heroin since he was twelve, and had the monkey hanging all over him. He was a pretty cool dude. Later, we pulled a couple robberies and served time together. "Yeah, I'm in. How much?"

"A dime a piece. Four of us."

Kenny collected the money and raced around the corner like a thoroughbred racehorse running off of nitro-oxide coming down the home stretch at Pimlico. Twenty–five minutes later, we were all in his room shooting needles into our arms, trying to kill ourselves with the ultra-fanny popping high.

Kenny would run like a marathon runner to the pool hall on the black side of town to get the heroin, score, and run back. Round-trip was twenty–five minutes if the connection was at the pool hall. We always worried if it took him any longer.

One day, I went with him to score. He made me stay around the corner on the white side of town, so the black dealer wouldn't see us together. He was afraid if his dealer knew he was sharing with a white guy, he would stop service. Kenny scored and met me on the corner. Four black guys, including the dealer, followed him. When they saw us together, they jumped out of the car, took his dope, started punching him from all directions, and beat him mercilessly for over five minutes.

Kenny wanted to know why they didn't beat me? They said, "You're the one that brought him in our neighborhood for dope; we don't have nothin' against him. We sold the juice to a black brother and now you want to share it with a white guy."

I helped Kenny to his feet after they left and took him back to YDC. He was hot, with a busted lip and black eye. He had a few choice curse words for me, too. I explained to him, that one of the guys had pulled a gun on me. Of course, I could see he had his hands full with the other three guys. He really did a good job defending himself against the odds. I jokingly told him, "It was brave of you defending my honor as a white friend." He didn't quite see the humor.

It was no big thing. I knew, after he healed, we'd be back to normal. As soon as Kenny found another dope dealer who wasn't so discriminating, we'd be back shooting up, getting high three to four times a week.

Every morning at ten–thirty, I made my way to the Swedish Massage Parlor to work. Proudly, I boasted to myself I had held a job for more than a month. Service became my personal motto, and each girl knew how dependable I was. But the more I became addicted to heroin, the less reliable I was.

CHAPTER 5

Ray Travelini, who had the fastest hands of any kid who walked the streets of downtown Baltimore, roomed down the hall. Kenny called him a born thief. He'd hit a store and walk out with five hundred dollars of merchandise in less than ten minutes. Simply remarkable.

I introduced him to breaking and entering. We'd catch the bus to Laurel, walk across the street to the shopping center, steal a nice car and drive to the middle class neighborhood of Radford Hills. We'd cruise around looking for houses with newspapers in the driveway or with no lights on inside. As soon as we came across one, we'd pull in the driveway and ring the doorbell. If no one answered, we'd walk around back, break a backdoor glass and walk inside.

Within fifteen minutes, we'd be back on the road to Baltimore, where we pulled the car behind Finestein's Pawn Shop on Baltimore Street. After tooting the horn twice, Mr. Finestein would come out, look in the trunk and say, "I'll give you boys two hundred dollars."

Mr. Finestein always asked, "Will you be bringing in more supplies tonight?" Some times, we'd take him two or three car loads of merchandise. One night, we had so much stuff the rear bumper on the car scraped and scratched the road every time we turned a corner. We filled Mr. Finestein's back room with inventory. I told him, "You need to have a clearance sale this weekend, because we're planning to bring you more on Monday." Mr. Finestein never laughed. Nothing was funny to him.

He knew he faced ten years for fencing if he ever got caught. How ironic that his store was located less than a block from the Baltimore Police Department!

Usually, we'd ditch the cars on Lombardy Street and walk around the block to Baltimore Street. I stayed and hung out in front of the Villanova Club until the late hours, harking customers for the club. Peedy Boy, the club manager, would step out and pass me a ten once or twice a night, depending on how good business was. Peedy Boy would say, "You're a street rouster by trade." At all hours of the night, the streets were filled with people. Obviously, my late hour work schedule kept me in constant trouble with the YDC staff.

Ray and I would ride the bus to the suburbs two or three times a week, and then we'd take a couple of weeks off. How we'd work was totally unpredictable. Sometimes, we'd get on a roll and go for three or four days in a row, clipping one house after another all the way to College Park, Maryland.

I began shopping the stores for Brook's Brothers suits, taking great pride in my choice of clothes, topping it off with an expensive pair of alligator shoes. I had an abundant collection of silk shirts with French cuffs, in which I placed gold cuff-links with diamond chips. Soon everyone on the block called me Vinnie. I liked it so much that when I escaped from the Brockridge Correctional Center, I used the alias Vincent Damian De Falco from Brooklyn, New York. (I memorized a map of Brooklyn with every detail of Fifty–Sixth and Eleventh Avenue in the Bay Ridge area, in case a conversation ever came up about the city.)

On the corner of Howard and Franklin Street one night, I ended up in a fight with a man who called the police. I was arrested, charged with assault and battery, and taken to central booking. A staff member from YDC had to get out of bed at midnight to come and sign for my release. The charges were later dropped, but the staff of YDC were exasperated with me.

A short time later, Ray and I broke into two apartments on Saint Paul Street. The police arrested us for breaking and entering. Eventually, the charges were dropped for lack of evidence. However, this was the final straw that broke the camel's back for me in the YDC program. The problem revolved around the fact that at age seventeen, I was still a juvenile, and the state didn't know what to do with me. Since I was only six months from my eighteenth birthday, they decided to emancipate me. For the first time since I was twelve years old, I was freed from the state system. I was a free man, but I had nowhere to go.

*   *   *

I moved in with my uncle. Years earlier, he had refused to let me stay, but after pleading that I needed a place until I could get situated, he let me move into his back bedroom. It was hard to figure out why I was always broke with all the money that went through my hands. It was now more important than ever for me to rob and steal.

I ran across some of the boys from Waxsters in the clubs, Chick Reese, Mike Mizell and Jerry "Bee" Coleman, all of whom were congregating at the Pumpkin Hill apartments, a low income subsidized housing which everyone called, "The Hill". Chick, Mike, Jerry, and I pulled a couple of quick break-ins to make a little cash for drugs. Every day we were shooting up, dropping pills, and getting high. We set up several scams for drugs in other areas, robbing the dealers of their money and dope. I had a small caliber pistol I'd slam in the drug dealer's face to show I meant business.

Because of my lifestyle, the stay with my uncle was relatively short. I found an apartment on Saint Paul Street downtown, next door to the apartment we had robbed. I greeted the people neighborly when I saw them as if I was a hard working member of society like they were. They never had the slightest idea I had scanned through their drawers, closets, and personal belonging two months earlier. I felt uncomfortable talking to them about their apartment as they related to me their experiences of having been robbed.

My apartment was on the second floor of the eight hundred block of Saint Paul. A narrow corner stairway spiraled up to the second floor to my room, which faced Lord Baltimore's Castle.

The first morning I pulled the blinds to stare at the castle, I felt mesmerized. The castle had been built in the eighteen hundreds, and appeared like an abstraction from King Arthur's days in England misplaced in downtown Baltimore. One could almost picture the medieval mystical feudal lords and monarchs walking behind the walls. The old dingy gray stone exterior was accented with two–fifty foot towers (called dojons) on each of the corners. In the center stood a monstrous moldy, dark-gray, brick tower with an entrance which rose two hundred feet to a small bell tower. You could almost visualize Merlin dancing around casting spells on people.

On the backside, I expected to see a crude water-filled ditch, with a drawbridge and a thick iron-plated wooden door that could be raised to clear the entrance. It was merely an illusion with the hard asphalt of Eager Street in downtown Baltimore running past the castle.

This fortified residence of maximum security housed three thousand inmates of the Maryland State Prison. The old castle had been transformed into a prison in 1811, and most of the violent inmates in the Maryland system called it home.

I had heard about Lord Baltimore's Castle for many years, but from this vantage point it was intimidating because of the size and medieval appearance. Never in a million years, as a kid eighteen years old, did I realize that one day I would be inside Lord Baltimore's Castle, serving time right along with Maryland's toughest inmates. To me, it was just a view from my room.

*　　　　　*　　　　　*

At the Hill, I met Butch Shecky, Charlie Sacks, Melvin Jones, Jerome and Pete Snow. Actually, I met Butch first. He and I were in jail together when I got busted on the breaking and entering charge at YDC. Butch was a sneaky thief with quick hands and slick moves. He could make things disappear on you. He was extremely versatile. He'd do breaking and entering, simple thefts, and robberies.

Butch loved to break in houses, but he seemed a little skittish in robberies. We did a lot of drug scams together, mostly with DC and Philly boys. We'd let people smoke the good weed and then sell them a bag of trash. Sometimes, we wouldn't even give them the trash. I'd pull a pistol and that would be the end of the show. I'd say something stupid like, "If you're enjoying living, empty your pockets on the ground. Otherwise, this could be a bad day for you." Butch and I thought it was hilariously funny.

Just to tell you how slick and quiet a thief Butch was, one night we broke into a house in Upper-Marlboro through the bedroom window. The couple was in the living room talking and watching TV, while we were going through the dresser drawers. It was spine tingling. The hairs on my arm stood up as the man went to the bathroom in the hallway less than ten feet away. Butch and I stood like wax statues by the door, without breathing, for several seconds when the man said from the hallway, "Honey, I think I'll go to bed."

She called back, "Come on and watch the end of the movie with me."

There was a long moment of delay as we watched his shadow frozen on the bedroom wall only inches away from us. The shadow slowly turned and said, "All right, all right," and returned to the living room.

We continued to ransack the drawers, coming up with an old Bulova watch which didn't work, a pair of gold earrings, and their clock radio. Mr. Finestein valued all of it at five dollars, and said he was more than generous. Unfortunately, some nights were like that, but most were far more rewarding.

Charlie Sacks hung out with Butch and tagged along with us occasionally. He liked anything that was illegal, so he fit in quite nicely. We'd go over to Melvin Jones's apartment, a black guy with a sweet tooth for drugs, listen to music, and do drugs 'til the wee hours of the morning. His flat became the place to hang out to find out what was happening on The Hill. If a party was coming down, Melvin was responsible for knowing about it.

At one of the parties, I met Jerome and Pete Snow. They were second or third cousins of Melvin's. Pete was the younger brother and hung out with us occasionally. His brother, Jerome, was a first class stick-up artist with a reputation of pulling a gun on you in a second and doing a robbery. He loved hard cash, and would go wherever the money was. He had the heart.

Pumpkin Hill was the spot. The boys from DC and Baltimore would come together at The Hill. They would party, do drugs, sell drugs and weapons, exchange notes, and plan crimes. There was little territorial animosity at that time. I drifted from my downtown apartment to staying at different apartments, because there was a misunderstanding between myself and a guy by the name of Johnny Weldon. There was a bad scene brewing and I tried to avoid it.

I was at my mother's house when Johnny arrived. I went to the bedroom and my mother answered the door. He started cursing and talking about how he was going to take care of me. I slipped through the bedroom window to the shed where I hid my guns. I pulled out my eighteen inch, twelve gauge, sawed-off single barrel pump shotgun, loaded up with three pumpkin balls and a couple double.00 buckshots, and walked out to his car. Johnny's eyes opened wide when he saw me, as I popped off the first pumpkin ball through his windshield, sailing past his left ear by six inches. Quickly, I fired the second and third shots in rapid succession past his right ear and then dropped a buckshot into his radiator. I drew a bead on him to kill him as he opened the door and started running. I was less than five feet away and could have blown his head off, but something held me back. I let him flee. I pushed his car off the road into the bushes wondering if he'd come back for it.

A week later, Johnny threw a brick through my car windshield while it was parked in front of Melvin Jones' apartment. It was fortunate I couldn't find him for a week, because I was furious and wanting revenge. Although I had had time to cool off, it didn't deter me from trying to find him.

I heard of a drug deal going down with Johnny, so I got involved. The guy was going to rob Johnny, but I asked to do it, and he agreed. Johnny came to the guy's apartment ready to do business, while I was in the bedroom with my shotgun. The guy said, "I hate to tell you..." and about that time I sprang out from around the corner and jammed the barrel under Johnny's nose. I will never forget his bulging eyes, looking down the barrel into my face. I continued where the other guy left off, "This is a robbery Johnny boy. Unload your pockets onto the table and walk out backwards with your hands up." I do believe that was the last time I ever saw Johnny.

*   *   *

I could never figure myself out. I was never totally satisfied with anything. All my life I had prepared to be a gangster, hoodlum, and a thug, yet, part of me wanted to be someone special, someone who people respected. I wanted to have a purpose in life. I was confused with a mass of contradictions of who I really was. I always felt empty, even when I had a pocketful of money.

As natural as the robbing and maiming was to me, I yearned for something more. Growing up without a positive male role model, I was always looking for someone to admire, someone to please. One of the men I admired was a small Greek businessman, named Peedy Boy, who ran call girls out of the Villanova Club. He was five foot four, chubby, mid-forties, and a nice dresser. He was a smooth talker with a ghastly face, and slightly resembled Danny Devitto with a gawky goatee. Peedy Boy drove a Cadillac Eldorado, which he parked in a reserved space in front of the

Villanova Club. Getting out of his Eldorado he would say, "Boys, let's have a good night, now, hear?" It was his own personal greeting.

Fat Steve was part owner of the Villanova Club. He was a real greaser, thin black hair combed straight back, weighing roughly three to four hundred pounds. His breath smelled like spoiled feta cheese, but he was the man. What I liked most about him was he ran the show. He had money and was in on all the action. He'd carry a fat wad of bills, four inches thick. All of his business was cash and carry. If you needed a receipt for doing business, you needed to go somewhere else.

Doc Saven, who made only token appearances, owned the other half of the Villanova Club. Somebody said his other interests were two other clubs on the block, the Pink Pussycat and The Big Top. Doc would sometimes call Fat Steve to see how business was doing, or ceremoniously stop by for five minutes or less.

Fat Steve watched the room like a hawk, accounting for every person who walked through the doors. He knew who was there, how long they stayed, and how much money they spent. From his view in the tower through a one-way glass front, he ate three or four hot sausage and french fries a night from Polluck Johnny's, the delicatessen next door, and watched the floor.

Peedy Boy had a call girl working for him by the name of Christy, who had a false ID stating she was twenty–one. At fifteen, she was a beautiful girl, with sparkling green eyes, long blonde hair, a soft charming voice, and a face that was drop-dead-gorgeous. She was Peedy Boy's money girl.

I can't count the times I asked Christy to leave Peedy Boy and go with me to Florida, or anywhere. I tried to liberate her, as if I was some knight in shinning armor exercising my solemn oath to morality. She deserved better. "This is no life for a beautiful girl," I pleaded. "Come on, just you and me down to Miami, where the moon shimmers across the waters of the Biscayne Bay. Smoking some good stuff, sleeping till noon. We'll dance till dawn. Come on Christy, you know you want to."

"No, Vinnie. Thanks for the offer. You're very sweet. You make Miami sound like heaven."

"Well, it is. Nice weather all the time. Parties all night long. You'll look beautiful down on the beach."

"No, Vinnie. I'm not going to Florida with you."

"Will you go to Washington with me?" I asked as sincerely as I could.

"No, Vinnie."

No matter how hard I pleaded and begged, Christy would not yield. She kept all my trash talking to herself and never told Peedy Boy. "Christy, you're making a mistake not teaming up with me."

"Maybe so, time will tell."

Time truly did tell. The last time I saw Christy was ten years later at the Excel Drug rehab center. Peedy Boy pulled his Eldorado to the front door and physically pushed her out onto the sidewalk. She was a human skeleton, weighing no more than eighty–five pounds. Heroin had eaten her up like the last stages of a terminal cancer. Only a trace of her beauty remained. She was no more than twenty–five at the time.

CHAPTER 6

Whenever I wanted to become Vinnie D., or Vinnie Divine on The Block, I'd wear the Maas Brothers silk suit, a gold watch, and imported Italian leather shoes. After I bought a new green Chrysler New Yorker, I was given a reserve parking place right behind Peedy Boy's Eldorado in front of the Villanova Club. I'd hawk for Fat Steve, jive talk people on the street to come into the club, always looking for that lonely guy who didn't have a date for the evening. The call girls were expensive. Nothing came cheap in the Villanova Club. Money was the name of the game.

I begin driving out to Prince George County looking for girls for Peedy Boy. There were plenty of sixteen and seventeen year old girls in Laurel and Upper Marlboro, who wanted to make some extra spending money for the holidays. One by one, I brought them back to Peedy Boy to work in the Villanova Club. It paid handsomely. Peedy Boy rewarded me by the night, and again at the end of the week, as hundreds of dollars were changing hands. My pockets were getting thick, just like Peedy Boy and Fat Steve. I carried a chunk of bills which I liked to flash, especially around the young girls in Prince George County.

Fat Steve would call me into his office, drape his big arm around me like a son, and say, "Look, Vinnie, you're a street smart kid. Don't do anything to mess up what we got going. Do you understand me?"

Fat Steve was big and sloppy, but he was the first man who ever showed a fatherly interest in me. Even though I knew he was using me, and I was using him, it meant something. "I understand," I told him.

He felt like he needed to explain further, "I help you, you help me, and we keep it to ourselves."

"I'm with you."

"I win, Peedy Boy wins, Vinnie wins, and the girls win. Everybody wins. That's what it's all about. Do you understand me, Vinnie?"

"Yeah, Fat Steve, I understand."

"Good."

A typical father and son chat? No! But it was someone I respected and wanted to model my life after. Maybe if dad would have shown me love and been a positive role model things might have turned out differently.

                    *   *   *

On Pumpkin Hill I was Darron Shipe, the gangster, drug addict, and thug. As well as everything was going on The Block, I'd suddenly just head out to The Hill to hang out with my old cronies and druggies. I thought it was something magical. But in reality, it was like a pig wanting to try a different mud hole. The mad, vicious circle consisted of my getting high for four or five days, partying, and staying wherever I could lay my head.

One Friday night while at a party getting high, Jerome Snow said to me, "Darron, you game for a stick up? There's a small restaurant in Silver Springs I've been watching. I need somebody to go with me."

"You checked it out, and it looks nice, huh?"

"It's a tight scene. Family house."

"Do you think they've got any serious cake?"

"Friday night is a big night for them. I'd be thinking around a grand." Jerome pulled a .32 snobnose out of his pocket to show me he was ready.

"I like the sound of that. That's worth our time. Let's do it."

"Are you packing any heat with you?"

I flashed the handle of my pistol from my front pocket as he gave a smile of approval.

Jerome and I drove to Silver Springs. At quarter to eleven when the restaurant was empty, both of us walked inside wearing hats and sunglasses. My heart pounded with excitement. The adrenaline began to pump through my veins when I pulled my.9mm. and shoved it in the owner's face. I put him down on the floor with a hard thud. Jerome grabbed his wife and dropped her more gently to the floor. Jerome's voice quivered with fear, "This is a hold up! This is a hold up."

I was sky high with nervous energy, continuously moving my pistol around the room looking for anyone hiding. Jerome watched them while I checked out the kitchen. As soon as I walked around the corner, a young boy, washing pots and pans at the sink, stood directly in front of me. I grabbed him by the shirt and shoved him up against the wall and began cursing profusely in his face. He was frightened beyond speaking a single word. His eye's glared back with glassy fear as he began to breathe hard for air. I came back to the cash register with the boy, and cleaned all the cash from the drawer while Jerome frisked the old man's pockets for a large roll of money.

We were inside no more than three or four minutes, made a clean get away and drove back to The Hill. We stopped at Jerome's apartment and counted the loot: Twenty–five hundred dollars, all cash. We shot up some heroin before returning to the party. For two hours work, including drive time, twelve–hundred–fifty dollars apiece wasn't bad. It was fast money…the way I liked it.

The very next night, we hit another restaurant in Upper Marlboro and walked off with another eighteen hundred dollars. Saturday night seemed to be the best night, because of the extra proceeds from Friday night. No one used night deposit back then.

I went home to Saint Paul Street, took a shower, dressed, and headed back downtown. It was great to be back on The Block. Peedy Boy said, "I've missed you."

I told him, "I had to take care of some business out of town, but I'm ready to hustle." He handed me fifty bucks to keep my interest.

I talked to Christy and asked her to slip out later, to go to a club in Laurel, have a few drinks and dance. She politely smiled, and said it was her birthday.

"Listen, that is even more reason to go with me tonight."

"Stop it, Vinnie." She said with disappointment in her voice.

"How old are you, Christy?"

"Sixteen."

"You're beautiful. You could be a model. You could be an actress. Is this really where you want to be on your sixteenth birthday?"

"Yeah," she snapped back, taking offense.

"You're lying. Where's your family?"

"They're around. I'm adopted. You're the one that needs to get out of here."

"This is my kind of life. I was born for this."

"Nobody is born for this."

"Is your family looking for you?" I asked, watching her eyes fill with tears.

"No, they think I've left the state. They don't care."

The words "don't care" summed up all of us. I wasn't quite sure what to say. Peedy Boy came over and said he was buying lunch for everyone at Pollock Johnny's.

Isn't that something, I thought. Peedy Boy cares.

✶   ✶   ✶

I called Jerome Thursday night and told him I had cased a place in Severna Park which looked good. The parking lot was full every evening.

I told him I was going to bring my sawed-off pump in case we needed it. If there were more than a couple people in the building, the shotgun would be better for control. We'd take a look at it when we got there. Otherwise, I'd bring a small pistol which could be easily concealed.

Jerome liked the way I thought. "Bring what you think is necessary, Brother Darron. I'm not one to put rules on the game. Look, if you think we need a rocket launcher, carry one. It's better to be prepared, than unprepared, when you're in this business."

Jerome and I hit our biggest payday, four thousand dollars. If that wasn't nice enough, we hit a small Mom and Pop store on the way back for another three–hundred–twenty dollars. We felt we could have kept going all night. We were on a roll.

It was the same story the next night. We popped an Italian restaurant in a shopping center, picked up another twelve hundred dollars, and I was off to change clothes. I drove to a night club called the Village Inn in Laurel, running across two old cell mates from Waxsters, Chick Reese and Dewy Bell. They were sitting with three girls. The one girl talking to Dewy, I thought was a good prospect to work The Block. I slipped Dewy twenty dollars for her. Three hours later, she was on her way downtown to meet Peedy Boy, who liked what he saw. She went to work for him that night.

Jerome and I pulled two more armed robberies before he dropped out of sight. I never heard from him again. Even his brother, Pete, did not know his whereabouts. I'm not sure if he got cold feet or just wanted to retire.

Some DC boys at The Hill had drugs they were going to sell to Melvin Jones. Pete and I went with Melvin to the apartment one evening about ten o'clock. We stood at the door momentarily before I calmly pulled my sawed-off shotgun from under my coat, and set the barrel next to the hinges. With a tremendous explosion, the first shot rang out, ripping an eight inch hole in the top of the door. I leveled the barrel to the bottom hinges and unloaded a second booming shot which could be heard in downtown Baltimore. The dust and debris filled the night air as I pushed the door in with my fingertips.

"Put the drugs and money on the coffee table," I ordered the two boys sitting on the sofa, who hardly had time to think about moving. A third guy stood by a stereo, and quickly emptied his pockets of hundreds of dollars before being asked. "I like a man who doesn't have to be asked to participate. You know I mean business, right?" He never answered. One of the boys sitting on the couch, pulled two small bags of heroin from underneath the cushions. I pointed my shotgun at the boy on the sofa, "Somebody's going to get seriously hurt, Chump, if you don't put all the drugs on the table. Now, if you don't think I'm here to take care of business…. Think again."

One of the boys on the sofa, again, reached under the cushions and pulled another bag out. "I like a guy who you can reason with." Pete picked up the goods and the money. We walked out, over the shattered door.

As we got into my car to drive away, it was obvious to everyone, including myself, that I was really capable of killing someone. I didn't care about my life or anyone else's life. I recalled my words, "Somebody's going to get seriously hurt," and knew I meant every word of it.

The next day, I stopped by Pete's apartment. A friend of Pete's, Scott Holbert, and his downstairs neighbor, Mary Hollands, were shooting up. I joined for a hit and we kicked back to listen to music. As I was talking to Mary, I realized her sister, Diane, was a good friend of mine whom I often visited and hung-out with during the day. Mary said she had been promoted to assistant manager at a fast food restaurant in Laurel. In the conversation, she brought up the fact about all the money they took in on Friday and Saturday nights. Sometimes it was as much as fifteen thousand dollars.

I said as an off-the-wall comment, "Look, Mary, why don't you leave the back door open for us?" I watched her reaction as she smiled. I could see I'd tickled her interest. She was the type of person who could be sold on anything that sounded good, especially if she felt safe in the deal.

"I'm serious, Mary. Pete, Scott and I can slip in the backdoor, pick up the money, and be gone in a matter of minutes."

"No. It's too risky."

"Risky? There's no risk." I countered.

"I've got a guy with me at closing until I leave."

"All you do is act like you're being robbed."

"You're making it seem too easy, Darron."

I could tell by her voice she was vulnerable. I fixed another hit of heroin, and it was a done deal. The four of us were set for Saturday night.

*   *   *

We circled the store twice, looking for any cops or anything suspicious. I pulled next to the dumpster and waited for the boy to open the back door with the trash. Minutes later, the rear door squeaked open. I pulled out my .44 Magnum, draping it next to my side, and walked up to him. By the time he turned around, I had the barrel under his throat, pushing him inside. I threw him to the floor, face down. Then Mary walked in and Pete dropped her to the floor with a hard thud. I held the boy down with my knee in his back and the pistol to his head, while Pete and Scott cleaned cash from the two registers in front. When Pete and Scott returned, they watched Mary as I grabbed the boy and said let's go back to the safe. He didn't move.

"Let's go," I shouted, pulling his shirt after he refused to move. "Hey, dude, this is a Ruger Black Hawk .44 Magnum." I shoved it hard under his ear. "When this thing goes off, there ain't going to be time for you to change your mind about going to the safe, do you understand me? The next person you'll be talking to is your Maker." I smacked him hard in the face with the gun barrel and I pulled the hammer back and pressed it firmly against his head. He rose slowly, and walked back to the safe. I filled the bags with fifteen thousand dollars, before putting Mary and the boy in the cooler.

As we walked out the back door to my car, I spotted two Prince George County Police cars across the street in the shopping center. We calmly drove past the cars, heading north on Route 1. It was a sensational adrenaline rush, as I watched the police cars sitting in the lot as we drove out of sight.

I enjoyed the write up in Sunday's paper, although I wished it would have been a little more exciting. Maybe I was thinking too much like a Hollywood movie with the three bandits busting into the backdoor with pistols drawn, tossing people to the floor, police cars circling the building on routine checks, as we escaped under a rain of heavy gunfire, speeding off into the night.

In the afternoon, we met at Pete's apartment to divide the money. I gave Mary three thousand, Pete three thousand, Scott three thousand and I kept six thousand. No one questioned my math or the way I divided the money.

Before the week ended, Mary and the boy had to go down to the Laurel Police headquarters to look at mug shots of ex-felons. The boy noticed someone whom he thought was familiar. The minute Pete was identified, his address came up in the same apartment building as Mary. Instead of Mary going along with what the police found, identifying Pete only, she got cold feet, turning state's evidence and spilled her guts about the whole plan.

Meanwhile, Scott, after fleeing the state, was picked up on a burglary charge in Texas less than 72 hours later. He plea bargained with prosecutors to testify in Maryland against me if charges against him would be dropped.

I was picked up June 24, 1974, booked, and charged with four felony counts of armed robbery and weapons charges.

*   *   *

The old deteriorated Upper Marlboro jail was one of the worst places I'd seen, and was one of the roughest jails in Maryland. The DC boys, Prince George greasers, hippies, rednecks, bikers, Black Panthers, and Baltimore boys were all housed in one dorm, appropriately called "the cage". Due to the overcrowded conditions, some inmates slept on the floor. Every moment tension filled the air.

Violence was so bad, the guards would not enter the cage to break up a fight until it was over. Someone would be laying on the floor and the inmates would walk over him like he was a hole in the ground.

The first day, I sat beside a big tattooed greaser, named Tommy from Bladensburg, nicknamed Speargun. He was in for killing a guy with a speargun. He had a big mouth, trying to be "the man" in the cage. I didn't particularly like him. I tried to keep a close eye on him as he was a real loony and could bug out on you any time.

We had a brief encounter in front of two other inmates, and he backed down. Speargun became less vocal after the altercation, but there was an uneasiness whenever he was around. I basically stayed to myself with little contact with other inmates.

Breakfast consisted of oatmeal mush with fried potatoes. Lunch and dinner, they served a thick gooey stew with traces of hamburger...the worst tasting stuff I had ever put in my mouth. The cooks must have had a contest to see who could make the worst stew because it never improved.

We were locked down twenty–four hours a day inside the box with absolutely no freedom, and no windows to look out. During the third week, my mother posted bond for my release for an October court date. Dad signed with her. He was almost friendly, but more than anything else, I could see he had a lot of regrets and personal failures in his life, and me being one of them. Although he never said it, I knew he didn't want to see his youngest son go to prison. Chip Wheeling, dad's closest friend, had told him tales of what went on inside The Cut at Jessup (the

second highest security prison in Maryland) and how some of the
inmates were turned into punks. Dad was scared for me.

*   *   *

I'm not sure what happened after getting bonded out. All the signs
pointed to the fact I was going to prison. I didn't care about anybody or
anything. I had so much hate inside me that I wanted to get even with
the world.

Every day I was on the run, never staying any place too long, because
no where did I feel safe. I knew I might have stepped on somebody's
toes downtown or on The Hill, and they could roll up on me any time.
I'd stay with Diane for a night, (Mary had dropped out of sight), visit
my Mom's for a day or two, and then it was off to someone else's house.
I was a fugitive on the run from house to house.

My final decline started at a drug party on The Hill, when I rolled
two guys for their money outside of Melvin's apartment. I picked up
Butch Shecky and we drove to Woodlawn Heights. We found a nice
house, broke in, picked up a few odds and ends, a TV and stereo, and
shuttled it back to The Block for cash. Mr. Finestein sold me a nice.357
Magnum, and I went home with Butch for the evening.

The next day, we went to a Woolco store and stole a brand-new color
TV, which was sitting on the loading dock waiting for pickup. Butch
slipped past the guards inside the warehouse and walked out with a
Singer sewing machine. We loaded the car like your every day "paying
customers" and drove off.

Early in the evening, we shot up heroin and walked next door to
Butch's neighbor's house. I threw a trash can through a rear window
and Butch climbed inside. We cleaned the house out, from the jewelry
to a lawn mower. In fact, it was so much stuff, we had to store some
items in Butch's garage. A couple miles away, I pulled my gun on two

people waiting for a bus and threatened them just for a laugh. I was totally out of control, like a mad man making his final debut.

We headed back to Finestein's to turn the goods into cash. For several hours, we drove around trying to find our next hit, finally ending up by the Laurel Raceway, scouting a place called the Clubhouse on Route 198. They had a parking lot full of Lincolns and Cadillacs. You could almost smell the money from the road.

Butch and I sat across the street in the car planning the hit, eating McDonald's cheeseburgers and french fries, waiting for eleven o'clock. Because of the layout, I was going in first to secure the kitchen and the back area. I told Butch, "Don't screw up, keep calm, stay in the front to watch the door and register, and let me do all the talking."

At five minutes to eleven, we pulled beside the building. I darted in the front door with my.357 drawn, shouting to the man at the register to freeze; at the same time trying to keep view of everything in front of me. After taking a few steps forward, I looked for Butch on my backside. There was no Butch. I felt like a skydiver jumping out a plane without a parachute. I glanced back through the glass door and caught a glimpse of Butch running like a deer in hunting season across the highway between the cars. There was no way I could control five people, secure the kitchen, and watch the front without some help. Turning, I said, "I'll be right back. Everybody stay where you are."

As soon as I hit the door, I ran for everything I was worth to the car. Seconds later, I was on Route 198 heading for Interstate 95 North. Screw Butch. He could have gotten me killed. He was absolutely worthless, an embarrassment to the crime community.

I picked up the paper the next day and read the second page headline, "Robbery Foiled At Clubhouse". The article read: "A young white male, 18 to 20 years old, armed with a pistol entered the Clubhouse on Route 198 at closing Saturday night. He held five people at bay several minutes, before fleeing. Police said, they were looking for two people. One white male had been seen fleeing across highway 198 heading east,

while the other fled the scene in a dark green late model car. An uniden-
tified source revealed that nearly forty thousand dollars had been in the
safe from Friday's and Saturday's business."

I was literally sick. If I didn't have enough reasons to kill Butch, I just
added forty thousand more.

I stayed down on The Block for the next few days as far from Laurel
as I could get, trying to hustle a few dollars. Actually, I spent more time
hanging around Christy than anything else. It was the same old story on
both our parts. She told me to leave, and get a life while I had a chance.
And I told her I would if she'd go with me. The whole scenario fell on
deaf ears. Peedy Boy was a smooth talker and, for some reason, she was
devoted to him no matter how he treated her. I could never understand
why she couldn't break away from him. It totally mystified me.

*   *   *

The next week, I ran across Butch one evening on The Hill. I couldn't
wait to hear him explain last weekend in Laurel.

"Hey man, I hollered to you that the cops were on the other side of
the road," he said without the slightest apology.

"You left me hanging out to dry with five people in the place. You ran
on me."

"Darron, I didn't run on you. I said, 'there's cops on the other side of
the road, let's go.'"

"You're a liar, Butch. I oughta kill you."

"Come on man, you think I'd leave you like that? Let me make it up
to you."

I wanted to take him out, but listened to what he had to say. He
knew a house in Howard County that we could hit, where rifles, guns,
and ammunition were stored. There would be very few problems,
since the people were out of town. My ears perked up immediately at
the opportunity of getting my hands on some weapons.

Off we drove to Howard County, pulling in behind the house, and breaking into the rear door. Just like Butch said, the house was loaded with two large rifle cases in full view. We loaded the entire trunk with rifles, guns and ammunition. Butch cleaned out the bedroom drawers of rings and a gold watch which he strapped on his arm. I warned him, "Get rid of it. If we get stopped, some cop might find out it's stolen merchandise."

Butch laughed, "You don't think they'll look in the trunk, do you?"

"Who cares what's in the trunk? With you flaunting a stolen gold watch on your arm, that'll give 'em reason enough to search the trunk." It was totally useless talking to Butch.

On our way back, I stopped at a small store for cigarettes. I went inside while Butch sat in the car listening to the radio. I struck up a conversation with an old lady who thought I looked like the Hemming boy. I told her I wasn't the Hemming's son, but maybe someday I'd stop by to see them. She said the Hemming's had gone to New York on vacation and she couldn't figure out why their son had come home early. The old lady even told me where they lived. This was too good to be true!

I went back to the car and told Butch. He knew the area so he proceeded back into the store for directions to the Hemming's house. The old lady was again more than accommodating.

Fifteen minutes later, we're trolling around Hemming's living room, taking TV's, stereo's, and an entire gold coin collection. The car was packed so tight, I'm sure people thought we were moving to the west coast. Finestein took most of the items and gave us eight hundred dollars. I kept two pistols and a rifle for myself. The next day, we unloaded the coin collection to a dealer for four hundred dollars.

We bought some heroin and cocaine on The Block and headed back to The Hill to party. Melvin had an apartment full of people acting wild and crazy. We pushed our way through the maze and dropped our drugs on the table to share. It was a mad house...music blaring, people laying out on the floor, guys shooting up in the corner, and a fresh cloud of marijuana hanging in layers as thick as a San Francisco fog.

My reputation as a thug and gangster, and always carrying a pistol, made me proud. Two young girls came up to me and wanted to go on a robbery. I thought it was rather strange that my notoriety was established with people I didn't even know. I rejected the idea, and told them I didn't have an apprentice program for juveniles.

Two nights later, I picked up Butch and we robbed a house in Silver Springs of gold jewelry and a high dollar stereo system. Butch caught wind of a drug deal coming down in Montgomery County the next night, so we drove to the place. I pulled into the parking lot a couple hours early to look around. Unbeknown to us, someone called the police and said a suspicious car was driving around the neighborhood. I walked up to the porch and was trying to see through the window when I spotted a Montgomery County Police car approaching. My first instinct was to turn tail and run, but I decided not to. The cops pulled into the open lot and stopped. I walked towards the officers, noticing Butch had hidden under my car. Of all the automobiles in the parking lot, he had to get under mine. I had a sawed-off shotgun, a.357, and.9mm. on the floor board. I told Butch earlier to make sure they were covered up, when we were riding to Silver Springs.

"What were you doing by the house?" the officer asked, shinning his flashlight with a beam the size of a headlight directly in my face.

"I got invited to this party," I said. "I was looking in the window to see if anyone was home."

"Do you have any ID?"

I reached for my driver's license, grudgingly giving it up, as he glanced at the picture, and then me. He noticed I was from Baltimore. "How did you get here?"

"Hitchhiked."

The other officer prowled randomly around the cars. When he got to my car he saw the barrels of my guns on the floor board. Then, he noticed Butch underneath the car, and that was all it took. He radioed in the license number and the car came back registered in my name. The police carted us off to the Montgomery County Jail, where two detective began questioning us. One of the detectives said, "Your partner's in the other room singing a song that you're the break-in artist. He's putting together a nice list for your resume. Do you believe me?" he asked with a devious grin.

I tried to stare him down for a moment, but the more I looked at him the more he reminded me of an overweight Richard Simmons. I wanted to laugh, but didn't. "No, I don't believe you," I said as defiant as I could.

"Come with me," he said as we walked across the hall. He looked over at Butch, "Now tell me again, how did you get the stolen watch?"

Butch's face strained with an honest look, "I was hitchhiking and Darron picked me up, and said if I liked the watch he would sell it to me. He said he stole the watch and those guns from a house in Howard County."

I lunged across the table swinging at Butch in mid-air, but the two detectives intercepted, and dragged me into the next room.

The following morning, I was charged with thirteen counts of armed robbery and thirteen counts of weapons charges in three counties. My court appointed attorney said that, if convicted, I faced two–hundred–eighty–five years in prison. I knew it was finally over. I wasn't sure if I'd ever be released from prison, just two months after my nineteenth birthday.

CHAPTER 7

I was held in the Montgomery County Jail without bail for four weeks, awaiting trial in Upper Marlboro, which was in Prince George County. The cells were nice, and the food tasted good. Afterwards, I was scheduled for trial in Howard County and then back to Montgomery County. By some freak incident, I was hoping they'd lose me in the system and let me out by mistake. Otherwise, there seemed to be little hope.

The trial in Upper Marlboro was quick and painful. The same judge, Horace Taylor, who had been my juvenile judge and awarded me to the state, presided. The prosecutors brought Mary Hollands and Scott Holbert to testify against me on the fast food robbery. (Scott and I were to meet again six years later in the Hagerstown New Jail). They fingered me as the ring leader. It took less than an hour to find me guilty of armed robbery, assault and battery, and three weapon charges. Mercifully, Judge Taylor dropped the assault and battery and weapon charges and found me guilty only on armed robbery. He sentenced me to ten years with six suspended.

The words echoed through my brain with the sobering thought of four years in the Department of Corrections for Adults. Painfully I turned around, remembering my poor Mom on the front row. Her eyes were closed with tears pouring down her cheeks. She had done everything she could to keep the family together, but had failed. Dad respectfully stood next to her, and appeared anguished to see his biggest failure in life going to prison. I felt he was the one to blame for destroying my life. He had taught me violence and hate by his own life, and now I was the one to pay the sacrifice for his work.

Two weeks later, I was taken to Howard County for a jury trial on the charges of stealing the rifles and gold watch Butch had been wearing. There were two young girls on the jury, whom I winked and smiled at during the trial. I figured it was my only defense, since I had been caught red-handed with the weapons and Butch had turned state witness.

When the jury announced the verdict of "not guilty", I nearly fell out of my chair, wondering if anyone had been listening to the evidence presented. As the two young female jurors walked passed me when they were leaving I said, "Why don't we get together sometime?" Both smiled, and left without a word.

Before the detective left the courtroom, he came over and said, "You sure had two guardian angels on your side today. You know you're guilty."

"Maybe so, but nobody could prove it to the two angels," I told him as I realized I had fixed the jury right under the prosecutor's nose.

I was taken back to Montgomery County, where my luck changed again. For the weapons charge, I was found not guilty in Howard County, but was convicted for it in Montgomery County. I was also sentenced to four years for robbery and numerous grand larceny charges, which the judge ran concurrent with the previous conviction in Prince George County. The concurrent conviction meant only four years running together on both counts, instead of two stretches of four back-to-back for a total of eight. I wasn't jumping for joy. Nevertheless, I felt like I had won a small victory, despite Butch testifying for the prosecution.

The sheriff's department van picked up twelve of us at the Montgomery County Jail. The deputies cuffed and chained us together with waist chains in groups of three. The drive from Howard County to downtown Baltimore was quiet with little talking. I pressed my head against the barred window, watching the last few minutes of my freedom fade away. The van turned down Saint Paul Street and we drove past my old apartment. I glared at the old homestead, remembering the day I stood looking out the window at Lord Baltimore Castle, almost recounting my thoughts word for word, "What a creepy, ugly place. How could anyone survive in there?" Now, I was about to find out.

As the van turned on to Eager Street toward the castle, fear engulfed me, and I wondered, what situations are ahead? Who was going to try me? What am I going to do if somebody tries me?

From inside the castle came a low, growling roar like disgruntle fans in a football stadium. The sound rippled over my skin from pore to pore, preparing me for what I knew was to come; three thousand inmates talking, shouting, cursing, all at the same time; three thousand radios blaring on different stations; three thousand men filled with hate and violence in the same building. It was a city polluted with a warfare of noise and discontent.

The van paused at the main gate awaiting clearance. The continued waves of noise lashed out as everyone on the van hoped the gates were sealed shut and would never open. Slowly, they edged open revealing the medieval, mystical abode for all of us to see first hand. The van crept to a side door and stopped.

Dead silence reigned as we departed, going up a stairway into a large reception area. As ordered, everyone stripped and placed their clothes and personal items in bags. A trustee showered us with disinfectant, like spraying for swamp mosquitoes. He seemed to enjoy his work, smiling constantly, considering it a baptism ritual to the Maryland State House of Corrections. After the shower, we were issued white jumpsuits to distinguish us from the general population.

The twelve of us were taken to another room for mug shots and to receive our numbers. No longer was I Darron Scott Shipe; I was now inmate #132534, a number which followed me forever in the Maryland Department of Corrections.

Seated on a wooden bench, we had a view of the five tiers and the rows and rows of cells. Inmates were hanging out on the gangway, leaning over the rails, standing around, going to and from their cells. The constant motion made it seem like a massive city in rush hour. No one seemed concerned about the horrendous smell of ammonia, urine and body odor which soiled every breath of air.

The noise of the old iron cell doors slamming shut, the loud music, simultaneous shouting and screaming was deafening. Some of the trustees walked by slowly, staring, and silently hoping there might be a weak one in the bunch. The guards held their positions, although they appeared to have little control of what was going on inside. It was another world...a place where a young nineteen year old boy would have to prove he was a man.

The guard ushered us past Cell Block A, which was for permanent residents. Inmates lined the gangway on both sides, staring, whispering, and making smart comments: "Got any plans for later? There's a cute one! How about a game of strip poker at nine tonight?"

Lord Baltimore Castle, better known as the Maryland State Penitentiary, which houses over 3000 inmates. The lower photo is of Eager Street and the entrance to the facility.

Keeping my eyes straight ahead, I tried to ignore their words. The guy in front of me turned and said, "There's Arthur Bremmer, the one that shot George Wallace." Mr. Bremmer turned around in his cell and glared back at the mention of his name.

New inmates were processed in Cell Block B and received into the system. After the evaluation period, they were assigned a permanent unit determined by the crime, and the time one had to serve.

Cell Block C was the last section, set aside for maximum security lock-down inmates. It turned out to be a place I was going to visit in short order.

The guard opened my cell, B242, which was the second from the end on the tier. The door slammed shut, and I felt safe. I looked the cell over as if inspecting it for approval. The concrete floor was old and chipped with decades of foot traffic. The thin, dirty, mattress had a moldy smell. The walls were solid steel with an array of bolt holes where an old, upper bunk had been removed years prior. The commode and sink stood at the back wall. Overhead, a 60-watt light bulb recessed in the ceiling, offering barely enough light to see across the cell in daylight. Off to the side a small window with thick, two inch iron bars offered a view of the courtyard and Saint Paul Street. I hated to look past the court-yard. My insides hurt being caged up like an animal. Just a year ago, I had been looking from Saint Paul Street to the Lord Baltimore Castle with no pity on the poor guys incarcerated. Now, I was looking back from the castle to see what I had lost. Pain filled my heart each time I glanced through the small window. Saint Paul Street seemed like the end of the world.

The following morning we were called in for classification, shots, and medical exams. Other than chow time, we were locked down the remainder of the day. In the next cell, a young guy from Prince George County was serving three years for car theft. His clean-cut pretty face was a real disadvantage in prison. Before I talked to him, I would peep through one of my bolt holes in the wall to see if he was awake. Often we talked late into the night.

One afternoon he got a letter from his father which said, "I'm disowning you as my son. Don't ever contact the family again." I could tell he was upset by the letter, but I didn't think any more of it. Around eleven o'clock that evening, I heard a thump in the next cell, followed by a moan. In prison there are noises all night long, so I didn't think much of it. But when a guard frantically rushed past my cell, heading to master control, I hurried to look through my bolt hole. I saw the kid dangling from the top bars of his door. His eyes bulged out and his tongue hung paralyzed to the side of his mouth like he had seen a ghost. I watched him for the longest time, unable to break away, until the guards cut him down. His limp body fell to the floor, like a spoiled piece of meat in a slaughterhouse. There was no effort by the guards to catch him.

*   *   *

Inmates within the prison served as exterminators, spraying for insects in the cells and hallways. They roamed the facility with total freedom, attempting to keep the rodents and cockroaches under control. A deal came down involving two guys in A Block who had ripped off someone on a heroin deal. A contract was given to the exterminators to take the two guys out.

The exterminators doused the two guys with the highly flammable insect repellent, and jammed the cell door locked while they slept. Within seconds, the cell exploded into an burning inferno. The blaze made a thunderous clapping sound, igniting from the floor to the beds. The reflection from the flames danced across the glass of the large window to the entrance directly in front of me.

I watched in dismay. A series of blood curdling screams could be heard throughout the entire prison. For once, all the noise ceased and only the death screams could be heard. The pair continued squealing like butchered hogs. A man in the cell next to mine shouted, "My God! Why don't you hurry up and die, man!" Their cries for help were a haunting curse of their destiny.

The reflection of the fire was so bright it looked like a sunrise coming through the window at midnight. Guards scurried to the scene with fire extinguishers, pumping water on the angry blaze, which seemed to intensify before going out fifteen minutes later. The smell of burned flesh permeated the night air along with the memory of the death cries.

*   *   *

Within four months, I received my first violation in an area considered off limits. I was on the third tier visiting one of my old Waxsters' friends, Freddy Cousins. When the guard caught me, I said something smart, and he hauled me off to lock-down.

I was thrown into a cell on the bottom floor, called The Flats where conditions were absolutely deplorable. The cold, smelly, concrete room had little light. The commode leaked a trail of water through the middle of my cell, running out under the door. A mattress, not much thicker than a small town Sunday newspaper, was rolled up in the corner. A solid steel door with a small 18" by 12" window was left open so the trustees could leave a food tray.

After the trustees brought dinner, which was usually bread and stew, the inmates from the second, third, fourth, and five tiers threw their leftover food, wrappers, or whatever to the bottom floor. It was a horrible, nauseating, mess with garbage strewn from one end to the other like the slums in a third world country. I thought it was a protest at first, but later found out they did it for spite, because there was no worst punishment the institution could render.

Within a few hours, the trash started moving on it's own. The little feet of rats plundered through the bags, feasting like starving hyenas, and scooting across the floor in a rage. The rats squealed and chased the smaller ones away while they ate, leaving bits and crumbs for the cockroaches and mice. Thousands of large brown cockroaches scurried across the floor from midnight to daybreak in search of food. This was my only entertainment for hours at a time.

At six o'clock each morning, two trustees methodically came through with squeegees and mops cleaning up The Flats like New York street sweepers. The stench had turned to a slick glaze as the trustees pushed through the goo, scattering the flies in a trail of ammonia and water. Everyone would be hung out of their windows, trying to coax trustees to do a favor. "Get me some drugs, man," one shouted. "I need some smokes," another added. "Can you get me any girlie magazines?" A voice came from the third tier. "Do you know Brown on B3? Tell 'em to send me some paper and pencil, I'm gonna write somebody about this," someone shouted on the second tier. The requests came so fast and loud that the trustees ignored everyone, and continued to push the trash to the end of the cell block.

Each morning, I looked around my cell and saw mice and rat droppings from the night time visitors. A three inch gap under the door allowed them to casually enter and leave at will. I asked the guy in the next cell, "What can I do about the mice?" He never responded. I held my small mirror out the opening so I could see him while I talked. He looked about twenty–five years of age. He moaned twice to acknowledge me.

"What's wrong with you, man? Not feeling good? Your girl run away with another man? I know how you feel."

I continued to talk, but I could see he was nothing more than a vegetable as he grunted back at me with the stupidest looks. One of the trustees said he had been in for five years and had bugged out, but the staff thought he was faking it.

Thoughts of the guy next door bothered me. The institution had won. A haunting, far-away look consumed him, and I could almost reasonably understand it. Sixty days in isolation was as close to madness as one can get. Pretty soon, the walls become your best friend and you feel comfortable.

Six months later, I was sent to Patuxent for more psychological testing: inkblots, multiple choice questions, and counseling. From there, I was assigned to the New Jail in Hagerstown. It was reunion time with the graduating class from Waxsters and the Maryland Training School for Boys. Most of the boys I had served juvenile time with were there…Chick Reese, Dewy Bell, Albert "Pineapple" Jackson, Joe Mondelli, Freddy Cousins, Jerry "Bee" Coleman, Snoop Johnson, and Mike Mizell. We had our own table in the dining hall; in fact, two tables.

Within two months, I was in trouble again. In the shower room, I was soaping with my washcloth. The guy beside me complains, "Your water's bouncing off me, man."

I was confident he was leading me into a fight as four or five of his homeboys were close, but my temper overwhelmed me so quickly. "Listen you, I can't control the water. If you don't want the water splashing on you, go somewhere else."

"You make sure your water doesn't hit me, man."

"You stupid, ignorant, punk." I said swinging the soapy washcloth and popping him in the eyes. He clutched his eyes, trying to wash the soap off. I pounded his face twice before retreating to the gangway, because I was sure the other five guys were going to jump me. Out in the opening, I had a better chance to fight and possibly get help. The guards intervened, and both of us were sent to lock-down for thirty days. After our time was up, we were sent to separate units with no contact. We saw each other in the yard occasionally, and exchanged words a few times, but nothing ever happened. I was put in a unit with Pineapple, Joe Mondelli, and Freddy Cousins.

Tension reigned daily with someone looking for a beef or someone wanting to get over on someone else. A guy named, Red, who was in Patuxent Correctional Center with me came into my cell one day. "Man, you owe me some cigarettes."

I told him I didn't owe him any, but he kept pressing the issue looking for an argument. He kept talking loud, knowing the boys on the
gangway could hear him. Finally, he called my mother a few curse
words. At that point, I kicked him in the chest as I came off the top
bunk, knocking him on to the gangway. I threw a flurry of punches,
connecting on every one, driving him down on the concrete floor. I
continued to pound him until his eyes rolled back in his head. Someone
pulled me off and pushed me into my cell. A group of black guys told
me to cool off. They started talking on the gangway how fast that white
boy was. "He got some fast ___ fist man, like a white Sugar Ray
Leonard," one of them roared. Another called me "Shorty Gangster",
which later became my nickname. One of the few ways to gain respect
in the institution was standing up like this which made walking down
the gangway a little easier.

*   *   *

In July 1975, I was transferred to Brockridge Correctional Center in
Annearundel County; a medium security prison located less than ten
miles from Pumpkin Hill. Some nights, I could smell the marijuana and
the Boone's Farm wine in the air from my cell window. The aroma
brought back memories of The Block, Christy, Peedy Boy, Fat Steve, and
The Hill people. As if it were some consolation, Charlie Sacks, from The
Hill, was serving four years on breaking and entering, concealed
weapons, and car theft charges. It was good seeing him again.

My second parole hearing came in August, 1975. By some wild whim
of the imagination, I thought after serving two years I would make
parole. It wasn't so much I had been an outstanding model prisoner, but
the last ten months I had done real well controlling my anger and temper problems. My counselor was going to attend the parole hearing and
address the board with recommendations. She complimented me on
how well I had been doing, reminding me there was always room for

improvement. I took for granted that she was going to approve me for parole. Boy did she sucker me in. She stood before the parole board and said, "Gentlemen, as Mr. Shipe's counselor, it is my recommendation that he be denied parole and be reconsidered one year from this date. Although, he's made considerable progress, more work must be done on his anger and temper problems."

I almost came unglued. If she thought I had an anger problem before, I couldn't wait to show her the one I had now. My first thought was how I was going to strangle her when we were in our next counseling session. My second thought was, it was too nice for her to have a quick demise. She deserved a slow death.

Later, she explained, "Mr. Shipe, you're making great progress. Can't you see that? You're getting much better. There are somethings you need to work on, and we'll be able to evaluate it from that point. Your next review will be in a year, and I'm sure you'll make it."

After I had spent half of my four year term, she said she thought I would make it next time. It was like she was a doctor treating me for some sort of infection: "You're getting better, but another year in the hospital and I think you'll be able to go home."

Another year of my life was valuable to me.

*   *   *

The first part of October, Charlie Sacks and I sat on the ground at the ballfield in Brockridge. Glaring across the field, we could see the dreadful Jessup Prison in the distance, also known as The Cut. The Cut was the second highest security prison in the state. This fortress, which looked like a five-story 1930 bureaucratic building surrounded by razor wire in the middle of a field, housed over two thousand of the most violent, habitual offenders.

"My old man is living down in Florida," Charlie said. "Before I got busted this last time, I spent three weeks with him. Man, the weather is too good. The sun shines when it's snowing here. And when it's freezing here, the sun's still shining down there."

"That's why they call it the sunshine state. Why don't we go down and visit him?" I said jokingly.

"Sure, like we're going to walk out the front gate," he gestured towards one of the guards standing by the bleachers. "Hey, we'll see you in a couple weeks when we get back from Florida. Can we pick you up some oranges on our way back? You know, the nice fresh Florida kind."

"Look, man, what have we got to lose," I said to Charlie, still enraged by the parole board's denial which had guaranteed me another year at Brockridge. "The worst thing that can happen is we'll be sent to The Cut." Although, we had heard rumors of how bad and violent the place was, it was only hearsay.

"I'm a gamer", he said with a loud, humorous laugh. "I've got another year before my second parole hearing. There's two razor wire fences to go through to get out." He looked at the two–twelve foot fences as an impossibility. He was quite sure there would be no way to scale them without getting our skin ripped to shreds.

I had thought about escaping for a long time. "I know how to get out of here, Charlie. Are you in or out?"

*   *   *

I prided myself on staying physically fit. I'd do five hundred setups, five hundred pushups, five hundred leg lifts, and run ten miles in place each day. I was hoping Charlie would be in shape for the escape. I encouraged him each time we talked.

I sold my stereo, my watch, and some clothes to other inmates to raise money. At that point, Charlie knew I was serious. I could tell his heart wasn't totally in it, but he was going along with me anyway.

On October 13, 1975, we were given our regular recreation time on the ball field. The bleachers by the ball field were situated a hundred–fifty feet from the east fence line between two monstrous guard towers. The bleachers had about a ten inch lip, which was on the front side of the seats facing the guard towers and ball field. Four inmates strapped us tightly with belts to the bottom side of the bleachers, under the ridge where we hung suspended for three hours until dusk. The belts cut deep ridges in our back and arms, causing numbness from the lack of blood circulation.

The upper photo is Brockridge Correctional Center. About fifty yards to the left of the guard tower is where Charlie and I cut through the fence and escaped.

The lower photo was taken when I first entered the Maryland State Penitentiary at age 19.

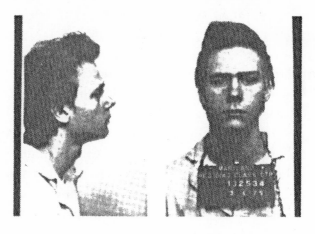

As the sun went down, we unbuckled the belts and fell to the ground. I grabbed the bolt cutters I bought for forty dollars from a trustee, who had stolen them from an electrician doing work at the facility. I ran to the fence, clipped two pieces of the wire at the bottom, and made a mad dash back under the bleachers. Charlie took his turn, cut two pieces of the fence and ran back to the bleachers. We continued to alternate, cutting twelve strands.

Voices came from behind as Charlie was about to go back out. We froze and stopped breathing. I tilted my head to the side to see two guards moving from one unit to another as they were relieved for dinner break. They walked on the sidewalk less than fifty feet away, never once noticing the twelve strands cut from the bottom of the fence, nor hearing our pounding hearts under the bleachers.

Charlie ran out and cut two more strands. On the next trip out, we'd peel the fence up, scoot under, and be in-between the two fences. We'd be vulnerable in the open for more than two minutes before running for our freedom.

I ran out first to snip the final two strands. Charlie was right behind me, and we both slipped under the first fence. Frantically, I started popping the strands on the second fence one by one, refusing to look back to see if anyone was coming up the sidewalk, or if we'd brought any attention from the guards in the tower. My heart raced with anticipation. We're going to make it. I could almost feel the deliverance as the last strand popped. I held the fence up to let Charlie slide under. He held the other side as I crawled to freedom. Neither of us dared to look back.

We scrambled through the waist high weeds and briars, running like human gazelles with lions in pursuit. A minute later, we hit a small creek, waded across, and began running relentlessly until we reached the railroad tracks a mile away. We followed the railroad tracks south, heading for The Hill. There had to be somebody on The Hill who would help us for the night.

After an hour of jogging and fast walking, Charlie and I reached Route 198. We jumped off the railroad tracks and crossed the highway. Twenty minutes later, we arrived at the Pumpkin Hill entrance. Charlie proceeded to several apartments of the guys and girls we hung out with, hoping someone would let us stay for the night. There were no takers, or they had moved. I dropped by Melvin Jones' apartment, and he said he couldn't take a chance on hiding us. So we stayed in a storage area for the night.

The next morning, we started hiking west on Route 198. Strolling through an auto lot, I noticed several of the cars had keys in the door as if they were going to start the cars and charge the batteries. I walked past a green 455 Grand Am running with a dealer tag on the back. I looked at Charlie and said, "This is the one." We jumped in and took off, heading for Interstate 95. A half mile down the road, I glanced back and saw a car from the auto dealership chasing us. I kicked it, ran a stoplight, and shot up on 95 South with no sight of him in the rearview mirror.

On the other side of DC, we took Route 1 and drove the scenic route, until we stopped at a McDonalds in Colonial Heights, Virginia. I struck up a conversation with a car load of girls and tried to persuade them to go to Florida. It was hard to believe, but they were only in the ninth grade. Charlie said if we got a couple of them in the car we would really be on a nationwide manhunt. Neither of us was willing to risk our new born freedom on two fifteen year old girls.

About a mile down the road, I pulled beside a new Cadillac Fleetwood in a shopping center and siphoned a tank of gas. In less than five minutes, we were back on Interstate 95. State police cars passed us in Virginia, North Carolina, and South Carolina; however no one showed the slightest interest in a car with Maryland dealer tag driving south on I-95.

*　　　　　　*　　　　　　*

As I crossed the Georgia state line, I pulled off in to a small town called Lavonia with a flat tire. There was a small diner and an auto repair, so I parked along the side of the building. We looked desperately for the locking lug nut to change the tire, but couldn't find it. We stopped in the auto repair and told the mechanic we were taking the car to Florida for a customer in Maryland. He said to bring the car in the shop. He would get the locking lug nut off.

When Charlie and I walked around the corner, two sheriff's cars had pulled behind the Grand Am, apparently running the tag number as a stolen vehicle. We calmly headed in the opposite direction. An auto dealership was about a quarter of a mile away. We browsed through the lot, but didn't see any cars we liked. The salesman came out and assisted us, even offering a test drive. The truth was, there wasn't a single car on his lot which would have made it to Atlanta!

We ended up walking three miles to a truck stop, catching a ride with a trucker to Tampa, Florida, where Charlie's dad met us. He carried us to Branden, Florida to stay with him and his girlfriend for a couple days, until he told us we'd have to leave because the risk was too great to hide us in his home.

Charlie and I caught a bus back to Tampa. We roamed around like two lost puppies, until we spotted a club called the Ki Ki Club, which had numerous high dollar cars parked in the lot. We strolled inside and had a drink, trying to get friendly with the local people by buying a round for the bar. It was eleven o'clock in the morning and drinking really wasn't my thing, so I told Charlie I was going over to McDonalds for lunch. Charlie had latched on to a guy who was driving a Cadillac, and said he was going to roll him. We were down to about a hundred dollars apiece and had to come up with some action.

I walked to the McDonalds and struck up a conversation with a girl in the next booth. About one o'clock, I returned to the Ki Ki Club to check on Charlie. The bartender said he had left with the guy. I tipped the bartender five dollars and told him to tell Charlie to wait for me, I'd be back at four. I came back later, but there was no Charlie. At eight o'clock, I figured something had happened, or that Charlie had ditched me.

I met this guy named Ray at the bar with two call girls and talked with him for a long time. Somewhere in the conversation he said, "Vinnie, how long have you been out of prison?"

He caught me totally off guard. I wasn't aware I was so obvious. "Uha, a few months. Not long."

"I've been out two years. Most felons have a rough time finding jobs when they get out."

"Yeah, you're right."

"I was fortunate. My aunt died and willed me a boarding house. Do you need a place to stay?"

"It just so happens that I do."

"It's fifty dollars a week, in advance. Is that a problem?"

"No, no, not at all."

I tagged along with Ray to his boarding house in Hyde Park. I was more or less prepared for anything. I wasn't quite sure if he was setting me up or trying to fill all the rooms. Surprisingly, it was a nice clean place, with no strings attached.

*   *   *

The next evening I met Tom, a friend of Ray's, who was a rough looking muscular man, with a large barrel chest, and iron gray hair combed straight back like he was right out of the 1940's. He and his girl got out of a new Chevrolet Impala. Ray introduced us, "Tom, this is Vinnie. He just got out of prison." He turned to Tom and said, "Vinnie, Tom just got out of prison, too. I figured you two may have a lot in common."

We struck up a conversation on the porch. Tom was checking me out and wanted to know what kind of crimes I did. I told him, "Just about anything…robberies, burglary, stick-ups, hustles, and pimping. I'm not afraid to do anything that produces money."

I could see Tom had good gangster blood in his system, because he seemed to like the way I talked. I could tell by the way he carried himself he was no slouch.

He said, "Look, Vinnie, maybe you can help me out. You need a few bucks to get going, and I need someone to keep an eye on my girl when she's working down on the strip. You know what I'm saying? I can't be hanging out down there."

"Sure. I could do that."

"It'll put a little cash in your pocket to get you going. Know what I'm saying, Vinnie? Come on out to my car."

Tom put his arm around my shoulder, walked to the car, and opened his trunk. He pulled out a briefcase, reached inside like he was pulling out his resume. "Let me show you what I'm all about." It was a handful of old, frayed pictures of him in the 1940's and 50's dressed as a gangster in a dark suit standing by a 1948 black Ford sedan with a submachine gun in his hand. There were stacks of money and bags of cocaine on the hood. Tom proudly told me he was the number one trafficker of cocaine in Florida. He had spent the past twenty years in Raeford Prison, and was trying to get himself going again.

I was impressed. Tom was the kind of guy I wanted to get to know. He was one of the big boys, a smooth talker and a big time hustler. From his gold chains to his diamond pinkie rings, I could tell he was on the move with action revolving around him.

He asked me what I needed. I replied, "A pistol."

Tom reached under his seat and gave me a snubnose.32 caliber. I liked a small gun, not too bulky, easy to carry in your pocket. Tom said he needed to watch himself because he was on parole. I wanted to tell him I needed to watch myself too, because I was out on a fugitive warrant for escape, but somethings weren't necessary to bring up.

For a couple weeks, I watched his girl, and tried to help her with business. Tom periodically stopped by, chatted, and dropped a couple hundred on me. Later, we got together with Dave a young seventeen year old kid who hung around the hotel trying to impress us with his criminal skills. He was tall, slender, and not very smart, just the kind of guy we needed who would go face first into a minefield if we asked.

We drove to Atlanta to the Peachtree Plaza Hyatt-Regency. I dressed in a nice suit and went to the ballroom to find older single ladies to dance with and entertain. Before long I was buying drinks, carrying on a conversation, and getting their room numbers. Excusing myself, I slipped into the bathroom, wrote the room number on a napkin, and left it behind the commode. Tom and Dave later picked it up, went to the room, broke in, and stole the jewelry and cash. Tom said, "We need to stay on the move; otherwise, it will be just a matter of time before I'm caught on a parole violation."

Finally, in a moment of true confession, I told Tom I was on escape. He didn't appear to be shocked or bothered, but suggested we needed to be more careful than ever.

We hit the towns on the east coast, Savannah, Columbia, Charleston, and then drove inland to Charlotte, Raleigh, and Greensboro. Against Tom's better judgment, I told him I wanted to drive to Maryland to see what happened to Charlie. We eased into Pumpkin Hill late one night, and I found Melvin Jones. He gave me the low down on poor Charlie. He had stayed out for thirteen days before being recaptured. From Tampa, he stole a car and drove back to Baltimore to see his girlfriend, Peanut Butter, a scabby prostitute whom he had been dating for five years. Charlie was madly in love with her, and determined to see her regardless of the risk.

Charlie ended up in a high speed chase, driving through an alley, bouncing off the sides of the building, finally, knocking himself out before being recaptured. He was sentenced to seven years on the escape charge, plus the original four years he had. Peanut Butter cried in court, and wailed at his sentencing and said, "Charlie, I'll wait for you forever, my love."

As a joke, each month after I returned to Florida, I sent Charlie a postcard of a pretty girl on the beach. On the back I signed it, "Charlie, I'm having the time of my life. Wish you were here. Vinnie." I felt like he deserved a little vindictiveness for dropping out on me in Tampa.

Tom had his own problem when we returned to Florida. His daughter announced she was gay, which was the most disturbing thing he had ever confronted. One evening while we were in a night club, Tom and I were sitting at the bar when the girl who was his daughter's girlfriend came over. She sat next to him and started mouthing off, "You're wonderful to understand the gay community's right to be different. Not many fathers would be this open to relationships of the same sex."

Tom finally exploded, threw her up against the wall, and pounded her like a deranged street fighter. Finally, the bouncers subdued him, but he had pulverized the girl to an unconscious bloody mess. An ambulance carted her off and the police took Tom downtown. Within two hours he was bonded out, and at my apartment telling me, "Pack your clothes, Vinnie. We're hitting the road."

So Dave, Tom, and I were back on the road. Tom knew people in every town. Because of all the years serving time, he had a detailed diary of his acquaintances and their addresses. We always had a place to stay, whether it was in Georgia, South Carolina, or North Carolina. Tom would find out where the local drug dealers lived and their schedules. We'd send Dave in first to clear or secure the house of any dogs or alarms, while Tom and I circled the block.

We forced Dave to constantly prove himself of being worthy to ride with us. He would break through a window or pry a door open, whatever he had to do to get us in. By the time we had circled the block, he'd have the front door wide open, and we'd walk in to steal the jewelry, drugs and cash. Obviously, none of the dealers was going to report a break-in. We had state police badges if anyone had ever walked in on us. Fortunately, it was something we never had to use. I always thought that it would be the lowest form of theft.

We continued to hit the big hotels with con games for the older ladies. Between the robberies and the con jobs, we accumulated a fairly large sum of money.

We drove back to Tampa, and Tom knew he was going to get picked up on the fugitive warrant. It was almost as if he allowed himself to get caught. He was comfortable to know he had a nice piece of change from all his hard work. He was sent back to prison to serve the remainder of his sentence, including the additional charges of assault and battery. I never saw Tom again.

*　　　　*　　　　*

I moved into a luxury apartment in Hyde Park, then flew down to Fort Lauderdale and rented another apartment in the Melrose Park area of Sunrise Boulevard. I opened a satellite office to work the beach. I'd deck myself out in a four hundred dollar Maas Brothers of Miami suit, silk shirt, silk tie, and Italian leather loafers. This was it; easy money, low risk, a real honeyloaf. Dave would come for two weeks, which he called vacation, score on a few hustles and fly back to Tampa. When the heat turned up a notch, I packed my bags, closed the office, and flew back home.

From Tampa, I flew out to Naples, Florida for a week. I worked a Hilton and a Raddison with a little success, but I never felt comfortable with the crowd. I packed my bags and went home. Staying only a few days, I had a restlessness inside I couldn't control, so I flew to Miami and hung out with a Cuban family I met. For virtually two months, I did nothing but sunbathe, hit the clubs, and eat Cuban food. I woke up one morning tired of the routine, wondering what I wanted to do next. My life was empty with nothing to live for. It was the week before Christmas 1977, when I decided to go back to Baltimore for the holidays.

I called a limo service to drive me to Miami International, where I caught the next flight to Baltimore-Washington International. As Vincent Damian DeFalco, my alias, I showboated a little in first class, buying the passenger beside me drinks, jacking him up with a lot of good trashy conversation. I had always been an accomplished liar, but I kind of out did myself sometimes. I had a Rolex watch, leather attaché case, a gold chain, and a diamond on my finger (all stolen, of course). He must have thought I was somebody important because he listened carefully to everything I said. I pulled out my wad of cash. It was just like the ones Fat Steve and Peedy Boy carried. I tipped the stewardess ten dollars for two drinks. When I saw the people across from me stare, I bought them a round of drinks and tipped the attendant another ten bucks. I was having the time of my life.

After landing at BWI, I caught a yellow cab home. It had been two years since I'd seen Mom. I stopped at a shopping center a block from the house and bought Christmas presents for everyone. Mom met me at the door and was tearfully happy to see me. Dad shook my hand, saying very little. I could tell they knew I was doing well for myself, maybe even slightly proud of me in their own way. I suppose I looked like a south Miami businessman, instead of a fugitive from justice.

The next two days, I spent with Derrick. I gave him his Christmas present, which was a lid of Jamaican Gold (which I had smuggled on the plane in the carry on luggage), and a pad of Zig Zag papers. He was ecstatic. We stayed high for two days.

I dropped in and surprised Sherry, staying two nights. I hung out with her, keeping a low profile, going shopping and bowling. The only part of shopping I enjoyed was going to downtown Baltimore for the imported leather shoes. I bought six pairs to take home.

Probably to ease the pain and hurt of saying good-bye to my family, Derrick and I downed a couple of tabs of acid in his apartment before the taxi came to drive me to the airport. An hour later, I was on a Delta jet heading back to Miami. No one came to the airport to see me off, but it was all for the best because my time of freedom was running out.

*   *   *

I landed in Miami on Sunday, and the following Friday I was on a jet to Fort Meyers, hunting for ladies with their hair piled high on their heads, driving Lincolns and Caddies. I made two quick hits, one on Friday, another on Saturday, and flew back to Tampa. I waited a week, and sold my diamond ring, the Rolex, a necklace, and an expensive watch I snagged in Fort Meyers. I converted all the small bills into stacks of hundreds for easy carrying.

I hooked up with Dave and we pulled two or three break ins, not scoring well on any of them. Late at night, we started rolling prostitutes on Dale Mabry Highway, picking up four or five hundred dollars a hit. We ran this off and on for a month, until basically I was burned out. I needed a change of scenery.

I called Rick Davis, an old friend of Tom's in Columbia, South Carolina, and told him I needed a place to stay. He had been more than generous and hospitable to Tom, Dave and I when we were working in Columbia. Rick served time with Tom in Raeford. When he got out of prison, his parents wanted to retire from the motel business, so they turned the business over to him.

Rick said, "I'm not going to do any special favors for you. I'm trying to lay low myself and stay out of trouble. I know when I was down, some people helped me. You're a paying customer just like everyone else, and you're on your own. Don't bring nothing down on me."

"Fine," I told him. "I need a new place to start."

I caught a bus to Columbia, South Carolina. As I was riding down the highway, I kept thinking of the emptiness and disappointments in my life. I was a vagabond. Even at the best of times, I always needed to have more. Nothing ever seemed to satisfy. I had taken the best drugs. I had stolen the best diamonds. I had piles of money. Yet, I was unhappy. I felt like there were no answers and no meaning to my life.

*   *   *

For the first month, I kicked back, trying to figure out who I was. What was my purpose in life? Why didn't someone love me?

A group of Rick's friends who always had plenty of drugs and liked to party hung around the motel every evening. Eventually, I joined in and became part of the gang. On weekends, Rick had a girl running the motel, so we could go to a fifteen-acre farm he had in Newberry. We partied from Friday night to Sunday night when we returned. I stayed back one weekend to try to set up a little action in Columbia.

Saturday morning Rick called, "Vinnie, come on down."

"No, I'm checking out a few things in Columbia."

"Heather asked about you. She wanted to know if you were coming down this weekend. She told me not to call you…so that's why I'm calling you. Do you know what I mean? It could be you and her."

I had been trying to get close to Heather for a month, and had not made the least bit of progress. I wondered why she had a sudden interest in me. "How am I going to get there?"

"Take the motel van," Rick said.

"All right, I'll see you in about an hour."

Before I pulled out of the driveway, I dropped some Reds, and headed out on Interstate 20 to the farm. About twenty miles outside of Columbia, my mind began to scrabble. I don't recall anything after passing a Ford van.

The driver of the Ford van said I passed him going sixty–five to seventy miles per hour. I suddenly turned and swerved to the side of the road, going off a twenty foot embankment. The van seemed to float in the air forever, even levitating to higher heights. As it fluttered through the air, a four foot round pine tree caught the van dead center, stopping it like it was shot down by an anti-aircraft missile. My body ejected through the windshield, hitting the tree, and ended up twenty–five feet away in heavy brush.

If it hadn't been for the driver of the Ford van telling the ambulance driver where I was, they may never had found me. The medic said I would have been dead if I hadn't gotten emergency care within thirty minutes. I went into shock with two broken legs and internal injuries.

Four days later, I awoke to an unsuspecting voice, "Mr. De Falco," the South Carolina State Trooper said. "You're a lucky man to be alive. Son, had you been drinking?"

I stared back, almost afraid to say anything. "Maybe, two drinks earlier in the day."

"They did a blood test on you, which tested positive for drugs in your system, but we didn't find any drugs in the van. Otherwise, we would be arresting you. If you've got a drug problem, you need to seek help. I hope you learned your lesson. I'm not going to cite you, but you need to be more careful driving. I filled out a report for the insurance company. I'll be leaving it at the nurse's station. God spared your life, son. I hope you know that."

"I appreciate it, officer. Thank you, have a nice day."

For three days, I sat around in immense pain in a body cast from my chest to my hips. I tried to figure out how I was going to take care of myself when the money ran out. I wasn't a member of an AFL-CIO criminal union which provided long term disability benefits. My survival was up to me. If a criminal can't walk; he can't work.

I called my sister, Sherry, and told her to give me the telephone number of Jerry Rhome, a state trooper whom she dated. I called Jerry and told him where I was and that I wanted to surrender. I was put under house arrest and kept in the hospital for a month, until I could walk on crutches. Then, two Maryland detectives flew to Columbia and picked me up.

*The upper right photo is
the Dodge Caravan I wrecked in
South Carolina. The upper left
photo is shooting pool in Rick
Davis' Motel. The lower picture
is in Tampa, Florida while on escape
from Brockridge Correctional Center*

CHAPTER 8

After exactly three-hundred-sixty-five days as a fugitive from justice, I was back in custody and returning to prison. I had enjoyed my leave of absence. It was like coming off a great vacation and having to return to work on Monday morning.

When the state police car stopped at the entrance of The Cut, something tripped in my mind. It was back to the survival mode. Some of the toughest inmates in prison would be around me night and day. Every minute of the day, I had to be on alert because violence, rape, and death are just part of the scene. Considering I was small and only twenty–one years old, I was more vulnerable than most new inmates, and I also had two broken legs with little mobility.

A photo of the driveway which leads to the front entrance of The Cut. The lower photo is me receiving my GED diploma.

As the electric gate opened, the car proceeded through the front to the west wing of the massive building. A mass choir echoed like a crowded subway station. When the detective opened the car door, it became that much louder. Music was playing from every cell, voices talking, men cursing, and steel doors clanging shut. It was the same old scene. While I looked up at the four stories of cells, I noticed some of the men looking out their windows eyeing me as fresh meat in the market place. Each cell was brightly lit, glimmering separately by a slice of wall between them.

I hobbled up the steps with my crutches the best I could, and was taken to center hall, which is the command post for all the gates and cells. I tried to take in everything at once, but it was beyond anything I had ever imagined. It was one big zoo…inmates climbing the bars like wild monkeys; clothing on clotheslines strung on the bars; all different colors of lights in the cells, homosexuals dressed like models; and huge men with biceps bigger than my leg staring me down.

I looked everywhere, down the west wing, south wing, C and D Dorms, taking it all in, like a foreign tourist. Nothing in life had prepared me for this moment. Fear of the unexpected and the need for survival gripped me both at once. Deep down inside, I knew I'd have to prove myself once again.

Charlie and I had looked at The Cut and talked about it from the ball field at Brockridge. It was much worst than anything I could have imagined.

I was taken to the infirmary and assigned a bed prior to being released into the general population. One of the trustees carried a message to Charlie that I was in the infirmary. The next day, he came for a visit. He had saved all my postcards, and looked forward to them each month. He said, "Peanut Butter ran off with some guy to California."

I tried to encourage him, "Maybe she wasn't the right girl for you, Charlie. It wasn't that you deserve better, but in the fate of all things the relationship would not have lasted."

Charlie told me how he had been captured, after only thirteen days of freedom. He was given four years for escape, three years for stealing a car, plus his original sentence of four years which totaled eleven years. I gloated a little because I wasn't given any extra time for escape, only having to make up the one year. I was back with three years left, and Charlie was sitting with eleven. I felt like the cat who swallowed the goldfish with a free one year vacation with the blessings of the Department of Corrections.

*   *   *

The next three months, I remained in the infirmary segregated from general population. An old man in the bed next to me had been in The Cut for forty–seven years. The state had decided they were not going to release this old-time gangster from the thirties, even though he was dying of cancer. Each day he became weaker and weaker. Finally, one morning he laid there like a mummy with skin as white as paper. Everyone knew he was dead as his death smell gripped us. The guards let him lay there an hour before carrying off his body. I smoked cigarettes one after another at the other end of the infirmary, pretending it didn't bother me.

I talked to a guy name Tommy DeFazio, who thought he was the gangster to beat all gangsters. He was a small guy from east Baltimore doing time for bank robbery, but was a good con man and game player. Tommy talked funny, out of the side of his mouth, like Humphrey Bogart in Casablanca. He constantly looked for someone to set up. I always kept an eye on him.

He said, "Shipe, I run protection here for new inmates coming in. You don't want to get hurt, do you?"

"No, not particularly."

"For a carton of cigarettes a week, I'll take good care of you, make sure nothing happens to you. You got a nice face, I can make sure it doesn't get messed up."

Here he was in the infirmary with a broken leg, after being hit with a bar by another inmate, wanting to run protection for me. I looked at him like he was crazy. "I think you need someone to run protection for you."

"Well, suit yourself, Shipe, take the chance if you want."

DeFazio was quite a character but we became good friends. I laughed a lot listening to him talk about how rough and tough he was on the outside (only about half of which I believed).

One morning, I overheard Leonard saying something about me. I walked over and asked him, "What's up?"

He replied, "You're a queer, you'll turn into somebody's boy when you're sent to general population."

I turned as if to walk away. When I did, I let him have it with my crutch beside the head, pounding him five straight times before the guard took me down. Leonard laid dazed on the floor as if he'd been hit by a stun gun.

"Tell 'em about that Chump when you get out of the hospital," I shouted. His cronies said they were going to get revenge before I left the infirmary, but Leonard didn't say a word.

From that day on Tommy called me "Shotgun". He said, "You're like an explosion ready to go off at the pull of the trigger." He did free advertising for me, talking out of the corner of his mouth with a heavy nasal accent, "Did you see my boy, Shotgun, go off on big Leonard. Beat him to the floor. Did it with a crutch. Hurt him bad, too."

Not long after the incident, Willie Dynamite, another inmate, was mopping the hallway by the infirmary. (He got the name because the top of his head look like it had exploded. What had happened was that something had come down between Willie and a couple of the other inmates. They had tied him down while he was sleeping and poured lighter fluid on his head and nearly burned him to death. The top of his head was a mass of scars and distorted skin.) Willie was a huge man, six foot six inches with a large burly body, and just as dumb and stupid looking as a water buffalo.

I accidentally stepped on the wet floor he had just mopped. Willie shot off, "What's wrong with you, small man. Can't you see I'm mopping? You don't walk on my floor when it's wet, boy."

I moved quickly back into the infirmary. Tommy came up to me, and said, "Look Shotgun, you're going to have to deal with this. He's trying to intimidate you. There's too many people heard him back you down."

"What am I supposed to do?" I asked.

"Just go out there and cuss him out, let him know you're not afraid of him."

I bounced back in the hallway on crutches, "Listen you, ____ _____, I'll walk where I want to walk. Nobody, ____ _____, going to tell me nothing. You got that scabhead. You talk to me with respect."

The guard rounded the corner as I was finishing. He broke us up, sending me back to the infirmary, and Willie down the hall mopping.

Tommy was waiting at the door. "It's all right, Shotgun, calm down. You proved yourself. He knows who you are now. The word will get out about you."

It was rather a silly incident but because others were listening, it told them 'what I was about.' Any sign of weakness would have made me vulnerable.

*   *   *

I was moved from the infirmary to J dorm, which had an open one hundred bed section. Each day for meals, one guard moved fifty inmates at a time from J dorm through the South wing block to the chow hall. The guard walked in front of a single-file line of inmates, allowing master control to open the electric gate when he approached.

As we were walking through a hallway, approximately a hundred feet long, suddenly an inmate attacked the inmate in front of him. He leaped on his back with his hand over his mouth to muffle the cry, slitting his throat with a shank, and dropping him to the floor. The guy squirmed on the floor for a few seconds before becoming motionless in an instant puddle of blood.

Everyone marching behind them side stepped the carnage, and remained in line. By the time I walked past him, his blood covered a three foot square area of the floor. Glancing down, I tried to avoid it, but my left shoe caught the edge of the fluids, tracking a wet shoe print for several feet. I scuffed my shoe, numerous times to clean the soles, but the sticky slick fluid remained.

I lost all taste for food as the guard looked back to see the corpse laying in the hallway. He calmly radioed to master control, "Master, we got one down between gates on south wing."

*   *   *

Tommy and I started running games on new inmates, who came from Brockridge for disciplinary action for sixty or ninety days. One of our favorites was crushing Tylenol 3 into a powder, selling it as heroin. When water is added to quinine, it tastes like heroin. The small amount of codeine gave it a little bite.

Another game we'd run on new inmates was to cut the corner off a twenty dollar bill and hold it on the edge of a folded one dollar bill. We'd catch a new inmate, tell him the guards were watching us, do us a favor, go to the store and get me twenty packs of cigarettes. When the guy would get to the store, he'd reached into his pocket and find only a one dollar bill. He would come back and try to explain the mistake. That's when we'd jack him up in a corner, pull a shank, and demand our money or cigarettes. (Cigarettes were like money, used for dealing and trading.) Most of the new guys would come up with the twenty dollars or the cigarettes.

Everybody had their thing, a game they specialized in for themselves. My thing was taking a pack of cigarettes and cutting the cellophane on the bottom. I'd take all the cigarettes out but four in each corner. I would then insert two pieces of playing cards, jamming them along the sides. I'd fill the middle with toilet paper and glue the bottom and cellophane back. I'd return the pack to the commissary and trade them on a different brand.

One evening after the lights went out, something happened at the far end of the dorm. The guy in the bunk next to me said, "Lay in your bunk and pretend you're asleep." There was a loud pounding sound of a broom against a body and the muffled scream of a voice barely audible. The bashing lasted for two minutes before there was a final gasp of air.

The group scattered, climbing into their bunks as if they were just taking care of business in their normal manner. It was only a murder. No one seemed to care. If it was something you were not involved in, you stayed out of it.

From the corner of my eye, I watched the guards come by for the midnight bed count. When the guards found the body, they quietly called on the radio for a stretcher and had it carried away without the slightest sign of concern. A solemn spirit hung around for a few days before it was totally forgotten.

*   *   *

A week later, I was sent to west wing because of an infraction. Sharkey Starlings, from East Baltimore, ran the west wing. He had been there for ten years, and the guards and officers worked for him. Anything and everything was for sale. If you wanted a nickel bag of reefer, it would cost you fifteen packs of cigarettes or ten dollars. A three or four day high of thirty darvons would cost fifteen packs of cigarettes or ten dollars. If you wanted to move to another cell, you paid Sharkey fifteen packs of cigarettes or ten dollars. If you wanted a female, you paid Sharkey sixty dollars. He kept twenty, and gave twenty to the guard and twenty to a nurse. He'd set an appointment for you in X-ray the next day.

My first cell mate on west wing was an old country boy named Lewis Diggs from Wheeling, West Virginia. He used to make me sick, listening to old twangy bluegrass music. From seven–thirty in the morning until nine o'clock at night, we listened to nothing but bluegrass. I had dreams of hillbillies playing banjos and dancing across the hills all night long. I wasn't sure how much of this I was going to be able to take.

One day, while he was at lunch, I stayed in the cell. I rewired the transformer on his radio, so when he turned it on, it would blow out the speakers.

Lewis came back, turned on the radio, and poof, a big cloud of smoke bellowed from the back. He danced around in a panic, pulling the plug, trying to salvage his equipment. I tried not to laugh, as he shouted to me, "Dareran, hep me, my dang muzik box's on fire, boy."

To get rid of Lewis, I recruited Tommy DeFazio to come from section F3 to rob us. (I could have paid Starkey, but I didn't think it was worth it). I broke into Lewis' locker and stole everything, and even took some of my stuff. Tommy took it to his cell to hide. I left and returned later, and as soon as I stepped on to the gangway, I shouted, "We've been robbed! We've been robbed!" Lewis came up about that time, and I turned to him, "Man, we've been robbed."

"What'da mean we've bin robbed, Dareran?" Lewis asked.

"They got it all. All my stuff is gone. They even stole my silk underwear."

Lewis didn't buy into the story. He could read between the lines and knew something was up. He put in for a transfer the next day. A short time later, he moved to south wing.

Tommy and I continued to hit on new inmates with our latest con-game as I was transferred to J Dorm. Somehow, Tommy pulled a con-game on the Clark brothers, Donny and Lonnie on south wing, which nearly got me killed. Donny Clark, the crazy one, came into J Dorm, walked over to my bunk, and literally picked me up by the neck and feet, and tossed me over four bunks. It was like something you'd see on the World Wrestling Federation. The six foot four inch giant, Donny Clark, coming in to settle a beef. Thank God, some of the guys restrained him, or it could have been curtains for me.

With eyes bulging and his face as red as a beet, Donny said, "Shotgun. If you're going to walk like a bad man, you better be like one. I'm going to tell you one thing, you better get my money."

It took only a short time to discover that Tommy had sold the Clark brothers a bag of fake heroin. When Donny confronted Tommy about it, he said he bought it from me. So I pulled my shank from under my bed and walked over to see Donny.

To prove that I had nothing to do with it, I told him I was going to stick Tommy in the gut for lying on me. Tommy got wind of my intentions, and took a dive which sent him straight to lockup. Not only were the Clark brothers going to take him out, but now I was after him, too. Several weeks later, I was transferred to E4, and Tommy was down in the flats on E1. I shouted down, "I'm gonna get you Tommy. You're worthless punk ___. Sell a friend out, you __ _ _ ___."

Tommy would holler back in his Bogart voice, "Shotgun, you'll never get me."

"The Clark brothers are going to flush what's left of you down the toilet."

"It won't happen, man. It won't happen."

Tommy was right. It didn't happen. From lockup, he was transferred to Hagerstown. Two years later, I ran across him in the hallway of the New Jail. We talked about the old times, the games we had played, and kind of forgot about getting even. It was always a game from the time you got up until you went to bed. Everyone had something going on, trying to out do someone else, or trying to get over on somebody. It was just a bunch of cons doing what they did best…to see who had the best game in town.

*   *   *

Early one morning, I was laying in my bed on E412 west wing. I heard a noise against my bars, and pulled my curtain back when I locked eyes with Leo Jones stabbing another inmate. I watched for a second, as the inmate grunted and dropped to the floor in a pool of blood. Leo turned and walked away as if he had resolved a customer's complaint. I closed the curtain and laid there, occasionally glancing over at the dead body propped against my door. I thought about taking my foot and shoving him away from my cell, but I was afraid someone would see me. An hour later, the blood had begun to dry on the floor, and the flies circled like small buzzards searching for spoils. Respectfully, I waved a towel to keep the flies from landing. It was the least I could do.

Captain Meredith pulled me into a room, investigating the murder. He promised if I would talk he would transfer me to work release immediately, and if I didn't, he would tie me in as an accessory. I told him I didn't see or hear anything. I was asleep.

As soon as I walked out, I saw Leo standing there. I walked past him with incidental eye contact, and returned to my cell.

For three days, there was a lot of tension, stillness, and quietness on the tier because someone had been taken out. I was the one witness to the murder, and I knew my life wouldn't be worth the time of day if I snitched. Leo was in for several murder charges, and even committed two more while he was at Maryland State Penitentiary. He was never going to see the light of day anyway, but I just didn't want to add to his scorecard.

Finally, after everything cooled down, Leo strolled by my cell one day and said, "White boy, if you need anything while you're here, you call me." He turned, and walked away and never spoke to me again.

Thank God, I never needed anything.

*   *   *

Ernie Miller came by my cell, and said, "Shotgun, don't go out in the yard today. Something's coming down."

"What's going on?" I asked.

"Don't go out in the yard. You'll see."

When the cells opened, I stayed back like Ernie advised. I continued to read a book, laying on my bunk, only half-way glancing up as the inmates filed down the gangway for yard time. There were only a few inmates left behind on west wing. Looking out my window at the yard, two groups had gathered at opposite ends of the yard, one from East Baltimore, and the other from West Baltimore. In a mass charge, the three hundred inmates converged in the middle like Roman gladiators in a war of clubs and knives. The guards left and shot the yard with tear gas from outside. It was like a Civil War battlefield, bodies scattered all over the yard, some struggling to move, some gasping for their last breath, and others left as dead corpses. Some inmates helped the wounded off the field.

Later in the day, helicopters dropped in the middle of the yard carrying the wounded to Ft. Meads Army Hospital, and to the Prince George Hospital. The death toll was five, with over twenty wounded. The war had been fought over a homosexual on south wing.

*   *   *

A short time later, I pulled ninety days in lock-down for stabbing an inmate on the gangway. Upon release, they shipped me to A1 Flats. I stopped in to visit Sharkey and told him to get me back on E4.

"Look, Shotgun," he said, "go on over to A1 Flats, and I'll get you back here in a week. There's a lot going on right now."

Sharkey was a busy man with a big operation, so I told him, "All right, man, don't forget me. I'll pack my stuff and move."

I landed in a cell with an inmate everyone called "Hippie". Since he was there first, he had the bottom bunk. I made my home on the top bunk. We seemed to get along real well.

One night we got high on marijuana and he started sniffing glue, which wasn't my thing. I climbed up to my bunk and dozed off. Hippie continued sniffing glue until the late hours. After bugging out, he took his leather shoestrings and methodically wove them together, making a deadly choker.

About two o'clock in the morning, he laced the choker over my neck, and pulled me onto the concrete floor. I squirmed to break free, but the leather shoestring was locked around my neck. I tried to pry my fingers between my skin and the shoestring but there was no space. I gasped for breath, starting to feel light headed. He physically had me in a position where I couldn't fight back.

Hovering over me, he whispered satanically, in my ear, "Shipe, you've got to die. I've got to kill you, boy. That's what I'm supposed to do."

I fought to my feet and reached for my small stereo on the table. I smashed it with all my might against the back of his head. The thud of plastic against his scalp seem to encourage him as the warm blood dripped down on my arm. I continued pounding and pounding as I became weaker and weaker without air.

The stereo fell to the floor. I then grabbed my coffee cup and hammered it against his head until it broke.

I heard the sound of keys down the gangway. I shoved him as hard as I could against the cell door. The guard saw the commotion, and shouted into his radio to master control, "Master, open, A110 on flats, emergency! Emergency!"

My body was limp as if I had only five seconds of life left, when the electric door unlocked and the guard entered. He cracked Hippie on the head with a nightstick, knocking him out cold. I struggled gulping air like I had been underwater for ten minutes. I thought I would never breathe again as I fell back on to the bunk, semi-conscious, only faintly realizing how close I had come to death. The burn marks around my neck remained for almost a year, to constantly remind me to never sleep or trust anyone in prison again.

*   *   *

They sent me to lock-down because of the incident, which gave me time to reflect on Hippie's words, 'You've got to die, Shipe. You've got to die.'

The following week I stayed awake, even though I was in a cell by myself, reliving those words over and over in my mind: 'You've got to die, you've got to die, you've got to die.'

Only when death stared me in the face, did I consider life to be of any value. I began wondering, where do you go when you die? What is life all about? Is there another life after death?

Time seems to put all thing to rest. Thirty days later, I was back on E4 having to pay Sharkey fifteen packs of cigarettes for the favor. As strange as fate may have it, I was put in a cell with a guy from east Baltimore named, Spanky Sparks. Ironically, Spanky's wife, Hope, was a friend of Mary Hollands, the girl who had turned state's witness against me in the fast food restaurant robbery. Hope was only an infrequent acquaintance at best. For some strange reason, Spanky thought I had a relationship with Hope before he met her. He put a contract out on me with a group of bikers (Wanna-be bikers, not the Pagans) for fifty packs of cigarettes.

Chick Reese, who I served juvenile time with, walked by my cell and said, "Watch out. They're going to hit you in the morning."

I slipped down the gangway and began talking to the guys for information. Finally, someone told me my cell mate, Spanky, had a hit out on me for the next morning. He knew my routine. He knew most mornings I would not get up for breakfast, so he was going to leave the door partially open for the bikers to come in on me.

I waited in the corridor outside the chow hall for the bikers. When they came out, I had twenty boys from East Baltimore and Prince George County staring them down. I said something to the one who was going to do the hit, and he said, "Look, Shotgun, nothing personal. Come to my cell and let me talk to you." I followed him, and he told me how Spanky had planned the hit, but he was backing out of the deal.

I returned to my cell, where Spanky was sitting on his bunk. I greeted him as usual, as if nothing was wrong. I picked up my coffee cup and with all my might smashed it against the side of his head. Blood went flying as the coffee cup shattered into a thousand pieces. I battered his face with both fists until he dropped unconscious. There was blood gushing out of his head and nose, flowing on to the floor as if I had hit an artery. My hand was bleeding profusely from the impact of the cup, slicing a three inch gash on my index finger. It was Helter Skelter, blood everywhere.

I removed the sheets from his bunk and mine, and used them to mop up the blood on the walls and floor. I then tore the sheets into to small strips, flushing them down the toilet.

In the morning, Spanky informed the guard that he needed medical care. He was taken to the infirmary where he received twenty–nine stitches to close the wound in his head.

*　　　　　*　　　　　*

Again, I returned to lock-down for the next three months, allowed out of my cell one hour a day. Most of the time I refused to even come out, except for a two minute shower once a week. I was content to be alone.

The first week I returned to general population I was in the chow hall and a guy named Benson Burrows came up behind me. I turned to set my tray down on the table, and started talking to the guy beside me when Benson sat in my seat. I sat down in his lap, jumping up immediately. I said, "Man, you're sitting in my spot." Benson snickered and shouted back, "Find another seat, sucker," to the laugh of a couple guys at the table.

I lost it at that point, flying into a rage, raising the stainless steel U.S. Navy tray to my head and bringing the edge right down on Benson's nose. The tray almost sliced off his nose; only a thin piece of skin above his lip held it on. Blood covered his face instantly. He tried to get to his feet, but I punched him once, knocking him down. Then the guards had me on the floor.

I returned to lock-down for an another six months, and received an additional year to my sentence for assault with a deadly weapon.

Nearly every day, there were fights during the one hour out of lock-down. Someone would start wolfing (starting a beef) with another inmate across the hallway during the day, and he would have to cash-in (meet the challenge) on the one hour of floor time. As soon as the cell door opened, they came out swinging like two heavyweight gladiators in ancient Rome.

Guards at center hall shot water cannons with a jet spray so strong it could lift a fifty gallon drum off the floor at a hundred feet. The guards manned the cannons and shot the flats, knocking everyone off their feet and back in their cells. Everyone would be locked in for the next two days until the action cooled off. Then it was the same old scene over and over again.

A tier runner named Mousy worked the lock-down unit. I paid him a pack of cigarettes a week for special favors. He would bring me an extra large piece of cake or an extra hot dog with sauerkraut, which was my favorite dinner. If I needed to get a message out, he would deliver it.

Although none of this seemed of monumental importance, I learned how the simple things in life are so precious once you lose them.

*   *   *

Six months seems an eternity in lock-down. But there was less tension because you don't have to look over your shoulder every minute, wondering who is out to get you or who is setting you up. (The last year of my sentence, I spent nine months in lock-down). After returning to west wing E4, every day brought something new. It was like the six o'clock news in a big city...murder, rape, assaults, and drug deals. During one stretch of time in 1981, we averaged a murder a week, assaults were counted by the hour, and rapes were too numerous to count. Violence was constant every day. Some of it I was involved in, and some happened in another section. It was my daily life, and I learned to live with it, like in a war zone.

Even the staff was not beyond the rim of violence. Officer Washington, a cool guard, was thrown off the forth tier for trying to stop a drug deal. He broke both legs and was out of work for a year. Another young tough guard came in with an attitude to reform the world. An inmate stabbed him the first week and he never returned.

Life has no value when you're around a bunch of men who have, one, two, even three life sentences, or fifty to a hundred years. Why should they care? A young boy coming into The Cut had little or no chance. He would end up being somebody's punk or a martyr victim within days.

I remember meeting an old inmate from the van ride to the penitentiary six years earlier. He said, "You've changed, Darron. I can see it in your eyes. You were a young man with an attitude six years ago, and now you're a violent criminal, institutionalized for the rest of your life. This is your life. This is your family. If you get out, you'll come right back."

I hated the thought that he might be right. On my last parole hearing they wrote: "Mr. Shipe is a detriment to society, and because of his violent nature, we recommend he serve the full term of his sentence."

The last two years I became a drug addict. The only thing which mattered was getting high every day to ease the pain, sitting on a bucket in the corner of my cell trying to kill time. I stopped lifting weights, lost twenty pounds, and became complacent.

One day while high, I started a fight with a new inmate who gave me a good whipping in front of the guys on west wing. I could tell the drugs had destroyed my hand speed and stolen my strength. I was embarrassed when I heard the guys talking about me, "Shotgun, got whipped. He can't take care of himself anymore. Too much drugs, man."

I checked into the infirmary as a drug addict, needing help, wanting to be isolated from the general population. I stayed in drug rehab for six months before being released and sent back to west wing.

*   *   *

On a cold, rainy morning in February, a sergeant came to my cell and said, "Get your stuff ready, you're moving in an hour."

I packed my few belongings in two bags, walked down the tier to say good-bye to a few inmates, and went to center hall. They loaded twenty of us into a prison bus with two guards, and pulled to the front gate. I looked through the window at the monstrous complex one last time, with mixed feelings. I felt sadness at having to leave the only family I had ever known: Guys like Sharkey, Snake, Slim D, JoMo, Junebug, Gunsmoke, and Joe Dancer. All of them had been there for years.

I also sensed a ray of hope at being released from the system as an opportunity to live like a real person. I thought, maybe I can go to Tampa, meet a nice girl, get married, and have children. I can get a regular job from eight to four, reading the newspaper before going to work. How absurd it all seemed!

The gate grudgingly squeaked open, and for the first time in four years I smelled the remnant of freedom. Being reclassified to a medium security prison was something I probably didn't deserve, but I surely wasn't going to argue with their decision! I felt proud of myself for having made it in one of Maryland's toughest facilities.

Two hours later, I began processing at Hagerstown New Jail. To my surprise in the hallway, I met Butch Shecky who had turned state's witness. You can imagine how excited he was to see me. My initial reaction was to beat him until he couldn't walk, but I waited to see what he had to say.

"Darron, what's going on with you?"

"What's going on with me? I'm pulling time for you dropping the hammer on me. You ___ __ _ _____."

"Come on man, I was set up."

"There was no set up. It was you dropping me in the grease, and you walking away free and clear. I want you to stay awake at night and wonder when I'm going to get you."

"Mary Hollands had already fingered you, man. That's what you got your time for."

"Yeah, that and you in Montgomery County with the stolen weapons. It's all right Butch, you're going to pay."

Butch walked off, glancing over his shoulder to see if today was the day I was going to get him. Anyway, he had ten years to pull for robbery charges he was convicted on after I was sentenced. If there was ever any social justice to partners in crime, Butch was receiving his due reward for his actions.

I was on the homestretch with less than a year to serve when I had an encounter in the chow hall my second week at the New Jail. While I was moving through the line, a guy asked me to pass him a spoonful of catsup. I had to reach across another inmate named Ashby Martin, to pass it. When I did, Ashby grabbed my hand and shouted at the top of his lungs, "You _____, you _____, you ____ _____."

One thousand inmates in the chow hall suddenly fell quiet. Even the guards stopped and stared. I felt every eye watching me to see what I would do. If I lashed out, it was all over for me. I told him, "I'd see you later." I took my tray and walked through the line to the trash can and dumped it. My anger boiled as I lifted weights for half an hour, and then jogged around the track to get myself ready.

I walked into the dorm, and saw Ashby rolling a reefer in the corner. I asked him, "Do you remember me? You know who I am?"

When Ashby looked up, I hit him with everything I had. His eyes rolled back in his head, and he went limp. With the next punch, I plowed his head into the wall, and continued beating him for two solid minutes like I was on the speed bag. His crowd gathered around as I stood up, and they separated to clear a path for me to walk back to my cell. One by one they drifted by my cell, saying I was a dead man tonight. Butch came by my cell, palmed me a twenty dollar bill and said, "Take a dive. They're serious about getting you, man. They ain't just talking."

Minutes later, the guards moved in and took me to lock-down. An ambulance picked up Ashby and whisked him off to the hospital. The guard said he was in serious condition, in a coma, fighting for his life.

He remained unconscious in a life and death state in a Hagerstown hospital. Sergeant Major Thompson stopped by my cell the next day. He always wore dark sunglasses with a toothpick hanging out of the corner of his mouth. His shiny boots sparkled like they were manufactured in a glass factory. He said the boy wasn't going to make it. He had two in-house warrants typed up with my name filled in. One was first degree murder and the other was malicious wounding. He dangled them in front of my tray window, saying, "The boy's not going to make it. Which will it be Shipe? You like first degree murder or malicious wounding?"

"Whatever. It doesn't matter to me."

"Blood clots on the brain is a serious thing. You won't ever see daylight again, boy. You're going to be institutionalized for life." His laugh was like a machine gun going off in short spurts, "Ha, aaa, ha, aaa, ha, aaa."

Thompson rolled the toothpick around the corner of mouth as if he was some small town Georgia sheriff. "I'll let you know tomorrow how he's doing. See you, boy."

"I'm all right with it."

For six days he came by and taunted me with the warrants, "It doesn't look good for the boy. He's still unconscious."

He never came back to tell me the guy made it. Six months later, I was shuffled to court and charged with assault and battery and malicious wounding. Ashby Martin was in court and testified against me. He was like a walking vegetable with brain damage and a serious speech impediment. He dragged his feet as he walked to the stand to testify, staring in the distance as if in a fog. The judge gave me another year for assault and battery and dropped the malicious wounding charges.

I was placed in lock-down at the New Jail for nine months, and then shipped back to The Cut as Ashby Martin's crowd had vowed to kill me when I was released from lock-down. I had left enemies behind at The Cut who were out to get me, as well. I avoided trouble for the next few months, transferred to Salisbury Correctional Center, then back to Brockridge Correctional Center where I first escaped six years earlier.

Over the intercom one morning without notice, the announcement came, "Inmate 132534, center hall with belongings." For eight long years, I had waited to hear those words. I was finally emancipated, ushered to the front gate, and given a fifty dollar check. I stood there for a moment wondering what hope there was for me, after spending the last eight years in prison. Who was going to hire me for a job? What was I going to do for money?

I walked down the road three miles, dumped all my belongings in a ditch, called for a ride, and bought a pint of liquor. I sat down on the curb in front of the store and got stinking crazy drunk, waiting for my ride.

DEPARTMENT OF PUBLIC SAFETY AND CORRECTIONAL SERVICES

MARYLAND DIVISION OF PAROLE AND PROBATION

SUITE 306 PLAZA OFFICE CENTER   •   6776 REISTERSTOWN ROAD   •   BALTIMORE, MARYLAND 21215-2343

(301) 764-4274
TTY FOR DEAF: 764-4034

WILLIAM DONALD SCHAEFER
GOVERNOR

MELVIN A. STEINBERG
LT. GOVERNOR

900 Walker Avenue
Baltimore, Maryland 21228

BISHOP L. ROBINSON
SECRETARY

WILLIAM J. DEVINCK
DIRECTOR

5/24/78

TO: Darron B. Shipe #132534
      P.O. Box 534
      Jessup, MD 20770

RE: Prison Parole Hearing
      Maryland House of Corrections
      Jessup, MD. 20770

Mr. Shipe is currently serving an original sentence of 4 years for
armed robbery. Since his incarceration, Mr. Shipe has received
an additional 3 years to run consecutive to his original sentence
of 4 years. He has received 1 year for an escape from Brockbridge
Correctional Center in Oct. 13, 1975. Since his incarceration at
M.H.C..Mr. Shipe has been involved in several inmate assaults
which has resulted in 2 additional consecutive 1 year sentences.
Mr. Shipe has shown no signs of rehabilitation and,we,the board,
feel that at this time to release Mr. Shipe would truly be a detriment to society. Therefore, it is our decision to deny Mr. Shipe
parole and to have him serve out his entire sentence.

Chairman of the Board

CHAPTER 9

Mom rented me a Plymouth Volare so I'd be able to get around. I drove to The Block in downtown Baltimore to check out the scene. A lot had changed in eight years. Most of the old crowd had left, and a new bunch had taken their place. The glitter The Block once possessed was gone, too. Fat Steve and Peedy Boy were glad to see me, wanting to know when I was coming back to hustle for them.

I worked the front door a couple nights, ran over to Laurel and found a girl who I persuaded to change her part-time vocation and work for Peedy Boy. It felt good having a few dollars in my pocket. But in short order, it was the same old grind, which left me dissatisfied. How much longer could I do this?

Driving around one day, getting high, I picked up two girls hitch-hiking. I asked, "Where 'ya headed?"

"We're going to Florida," one replied.

Something tripped in my mind, like a divine revelation, when she said Florida. That was the answer! I could go to Florida and resurrect the old Vinnie. "You're kiddin'. That's where I'm going," I blurted out. "This is unreal!"

"Are you serious?" she asked, having heard that line before.

"Serious? I'm serious. I'm heading for Florida. Tampa." Without a second thought, they jumped in the car and we're headed south. I didn't bother to stop by the house to get my toothbrush or a change of clothes.

I did call Mom from a truck stop in North Carolina and told her I would be gone for a few days. I had no idea it would be a year later before I returned.

We breezed in to Columbia, South Carolina, to visit Tom's old friend, Rick Davis. We stayed with him two days, partying, and doing drugs, until the girls got antsy and wanted to hit the road.

By six o'clock the next day, we were in downtown Atlanta. I surveyed the city with disappointment. The mystique had disappeared; nothing looked the same as it had six years ago. I parked at the corner of Peachtree and Piedmont, across from the bus station, a real action packed area at one time. The girls stood by the car while I went into the Blue Lagoon Club. For early evening, a nice crowd was hanging out watching a college football game.

I had convinced the youngest girl to work on the street so we could pick up some money. She was a pretty girl from Ridgley Park, Maryland, with a soft sensuous voice and long blondish–brown hair. The other girl didn't want any of the action.

I got in to an argument with another hustler in front of the club which was something I didn't need. He and I had some heated words and I told the girls to get in the car. We took off, and the guy jumped into a cab to follow us, which was one of the screwiest things I've ever encountered. The cab stayed on my bumper for over a mile as I tried to lose him in the downtown traffic, which was impossible. Coming up to the I-75 and I-85 interchange, I noticed the cab abruptly turned off the entrance ramp. Almost immediately, another car pulled in behind and tailgated us. I punched it, and started running away from the car going up on the ramp when the blue flashing lights came on behind. Evidently, the cab saw the uncover police car and turned off, leaving the cops on our tail.

From nowhere, a police van came along side, and rammed us into the concrete retainer wall, tearing the entire right side of the car to pieces. The car ground to a stop against the wall with two of Atlanta's finest police officers charging toward the car with revolvers drawn, aimed at me.

*   *   *

Of all things, I couldn't find my driver's license. They said they had me under surveillance on Piedmont Street. I tried to explain, "If you had me under surveillance you saw the taxi chasing us, I just was trying to get away. I didn't want any trouble."

They released the girls, but arrested me. The next morning, I stood before the magistrate who set bond at four hundred dollars. After the girls bailed me out, we walked to the bus terminal and bought three tickets to Macon, Georgia, which left us with twelve dollars. Macon turned out to be a waste of time, for absolutely nothing was happening in the city as we walked the streets trying to find some action.

Nearly broke after dinner, I rolled a guy for enough money for three bus tickets to Tampa and ended up with a few dollars left. This was the first crime I had committed since being released from prison. It felt good to get back in the groove.

Tampa had changed drastically. The old place, the Ki Ki Club where I used to hang out was torn down. I caught a bus to Ray's apartment in Hyde Park but he had moved. I tried to find Dave, but no one even knew him. It was like waking up in a bad dream. I was so disappointed I would rather have been back in prison. At least the old-timers remained from year to year!

Dale Mabry Highway was alive, but had a different breed of people working it. I wasn't sure I could fit in with what was happening. The girls and I separated. The young pretty girl went off with a guy to Miami, and the other girl headed in another direction. It was really good because I preferred working alone, not worrying about other people.

I felt lonely on the streets with no friends. I went to a park and sat on a bench, staring out across the water, wondering what to do next. I had wrecked the rental car, my family was disappointed in me, and I had let my mother down for the thousandth time. With only eight dollars in my pocket and no place to stay, I was at my wits end. Since getting out of prison, life was a dead end.

Somehow, I felt fate put people in my path to help me during my lowest times. On this day, a young girl walked past me while I sat on the park bench. I said something to her, and the next thing I knew she took me home for the evening.

Marsey Hutton had a nice little home on Swananee Avenue. The girl's dad had plenty of money. Twice a month, he'd drop a check in the mail to help her with expenses. This was too good to be true! I talked her and another girl into hustling on the streets. We worked out of the Holiday Inn bar where a lot of businessmen stayed. For awhile, we made good money and I was eating steak every night, but I should have known it was too good to be true. Marsey was extremely jealous, and something came up between her and the other girl. The next thing I knew she beat up the other girl, and threw me out on the street. I tried to reason with her, but she was not interested in hearing any of my stories.

I wandered over to a park and met a drug dealer I'd been dealing with recently. I was going to purchase an ounce of dope to get high, and put Marsey behind me. After seeing his wad of money, I decided to roll him. I sucker punched him with a hard right hook, breaking his jaw, knocking him slam out. I grabbed the dope and the cash and ran to a friend's house.

No sooner had I sat down in a chair, than two Tampa police officers knocked twice on the door. Then suddenly, without warning, the door came crashing down. I threw my leather jacket over my face and dove through a picture window onto the lawn. After hearing the sound of glass shattering, I heard three shots fired in rapid succession, striking the window molding. A female officer grabbed me by the arm; I threw a glancing punch which barely struck the side of her head. She countered with a direct hit of her nightstick to the back of my head, laying me out cold.

*   *   *

Vincent Damian DeFalco had no previous arrest, and was sentenced to thirty days for a class B misdemeanor (to me this was like a weekend sentence). Frank Constantino, a former big time gangster, dropped by and talked with me. He said he'd been saved and set free of his old lifestyle while serving time in Glades Correctional Institution. He persistently kept telling me how Jesus Christ changed his life, made him a new creature and filled the emptiness in his life. The old lifestyle was death and destruction.

I tried to be respectful, listening, but I just couldn't see the religious thing in my life. I'm sure he meant well; but that was his thing, not mine. After I made a comment that I wasn't interested he said, "I'll be praying for you that someday you'll open your heart up to receive the truth about Jesus Christ. One day, you'll have to decide who He is."

I told him, "Fine, but not now. I'll wait until later to find out who Jesus is."

Twenty days later I was released from the Tampa City Jail, along with a drug addict named Lawrence. Lawrence had suffered a stroke while taking heroin, resulting in the entire left side of his body being partially paralyzed. When he walked, he dragged his left foot behind him, and his left arm dangled by his side.

Lawrence knew all the drug pushers in town, which I counted as a high attribute. One evening, we went to a dealer's house on the outskirts of Tampa, and pounded on the door for ten minutes. The guy wouldn't wake up. I hollered, tapped on the window, threw a rock at the side of the house, but he continued to sleep. I could see him through the bedroom window, apparently he was zonked out. So I took off my jacket, placed it over the backdoor window, popped it out, and we were inside.

Lawrence liked VCR's, electronic gadgets, and junk that was easy to sell but hard to carry. I went right to the bedroom for the cash. On his night stand was a big thick wad of bills, a diamond ring, and a gold chain. He was snoring like a pig in a pile of garbage. At the exact moment I reached across his body to get the wad of cash, Lawrence dropped the stereo in the living room. The sleeping dealer's eyes popped open. Staring at me for a second before grabbing my hand, he forced me to start punching him with my free hand. We had knocked on his door and window for ten minutes, and he had not moved a muscle. Now with a little thud in the living room, the guy instantly awoke. I had his money, but he fought hard to break it loose.

I could hear Lawrence making his slow, sauntering way to the door with some stuff. I pounded the guy with one hand and held on to the money with the other, trying to give Lawrence reasonable time to escape. It seemed like an eternity before I heard the car start. I pushed the guy against the wall, and I ran out the front door as Lawrence was pulling off. Running like a wild jack rabbit, I latched on the door handle, barely able to get in as he sped away.

*   *   *

I rented an efficiency apartment at the Floridan Hotel. Lawrence visited daily, bringing his heroin and coke. I felt more and more as if he had become a leech. Reluctantly, I continued to pull small jobs and robberies with him. I personally didn't have anything against handicapped people, but his disability posed a definite problem in a getaway.

One evening, he set up a drug deal with a girl outside a bar. If she had not been so flashy with the cash, I probably would never have robbed her, for I had no intentions. She pulled a bag of Black Beauties out of her pocket to sell me a quarter's worth, and the next thing I knew, I plowed her right in the temple. She went sprawling against the side of the brick building like the Roadrunner hitting the side of a mountain. I took the Beauties and her three hundred dollars, and casually walked off.

The next day, Lawrence was arrested for robbery and breaking and entering. I braced myself, thinking he'd drop me in the grease and I would end up with charges. To my surprise, nothing ever happened. Lawrence went down alone.

A few days later, while cruising Dale Mabry Highway, I stopped in a country western bar. I sat at the bar next to a nice looking blonde and began flirting, trying to make conversation, which she totally ignored. Finally, out of the blue, she warmed up with small talk, and then invited me to come home with her. I was astonished.

Two days later, I moved in with Linda Davidson in a small town called Seffner, Florida about ten miles east of Tampa. In the morning, she'd go to work while I hit Dale Mabry Highway to hustle. I scurried the block, looking for wayward strangers, tourists, lonely housewives, drug scores, and easy takes. It was business as usual. For some unknown reason, I imposed a self-moratorium on robberies and break-in's. As thrilling as robberies and break-in's used to be for me, I didn't have the heart for them anymore.

Linda started talking marriage, and took me to Orlando to meet her parents. Her dad had a gun collection and we hit it off great. Her mother was a different story. She knew something wasn't right with me. She would take Linda off to the side and talk about me. Linda revealed her mother's reservations and doubts: I didn't have a job. I wasn't a Catholic, and I looked like her ex-husband. Her mother knew we were on a train going nowhere and that I just wasn't her daughter's type.

One morning, Linda and I said our good-byes, and she took me to the bus terminal in downtown Tampa. I caught the first Trailway bus heading north.

I constantly looked for something I seemed to have lost. I could never find what I was searching for in life. A huge hole in the middle of my heart made me feel so empty. I thought if I could just get back to

Florida, maybe I'd recapture the old Vinnie and be satisfied. I searched and searched for Vinnie, but I couldn't find him. He was dead, in the past somewhere, never to return again.

*   *   *

Upon arriving in Baltimore, I remembered how disappointed my Mom and the rest of my family was with me. After wrecking the rental car and costing her so much money, my dad didn't want her to have any further contact with me. A year had passed since I left. Of all the mind games I played with other people, the biggest one was the one I played with myself…that I was going to be able to make it in life.

One of the first places I went to was the Villanova Club. Fat Steve and Peedy Boy were glad to see me, wondering where I had been for the past year. As always, they were prospering. Peedy Boy pulled a lump of bills from his pocket, "Are you ready to do a little hustling, Vinnie? Money, money, money."

"Yeah, I'm back. I need to make some cash."

"Get me some girls."

I said sure, but that didn't even make sense to me. I didn't have the heart for The Block.

Christy came in, and I could see she was strung out. She'd been shooting heroin for awhile and it showed drastically on her face. Her eyes were sunk deep in to her face with lines of heaviness. This once gorgeous girl was now only pretty. I told her, she had missed out on going to Florida with me. She was so spaced out she didn't even know who I was, although she pretended to know me. She probably thought I was just another customer.

I drove a borrowed car back to mom's house, really down and depressed. She had a tool shed in the back yard where I kept my weapons, a sawed-off shotgun, a .32 snobnose, a 30-30 rifle, and a .22 caliber rifle. I sat on the floor of the tool shed, cleaning my shotgun, thinking of how I was twenty–nine years old and didn't have anything going for myself. I had traveled to Florida looking for someone who didn't even exist, trying to live a life of someone in the past. All the hopes and dreams I had when I got out of prison were gone. And now, it was another failure in my life. I just wanted to cry because I was a nobody, and felt I would never be any-body. My life had become a total waste.

I returned to the house and dressed in a nice gold silk shirt with my cream colored Maas Brothers suit and top coat. I decided I was going out like a gangster; at least the guys in The Cut would be reading about me in tomorrow's headlines. I didn't have anything to live for. There was no hope, no future, and no family. I was going out to rob everything in sight. When I got cornered by the cops, I'd shoot it out. I'd kill as many people as I could. Sharkey, Junebug, and Joe Dancer would read how Shotgun went out like a gangster in a blaze of glory. They would be proud, talking about me with fond memories in the cell block: "You remember Shotgun, don't you? Over on E412, west wing…small white boy that hated everybody? That's him. He made the papers. Shot up some people downtown. Crazy ___."

I was around the corner of the tool shed putting on the shoulder hol-ster for my shotgun, loading my pockets with ammunition, when I noticed my mom coming out onto the back porch. Sitting down in her favorite rocking chair, she held her old worn Bible in her lap and appeared to be praying. I watched her sitting there, so peaceful and calm, having no idea what new troubles I was about to bring her way in the next few hours.

I felt sorry for her. She had tried so hard in life to make things right for everyone. Yet, I could never be a son she would be proud of in life. I was the one who disgraced her in front of her neighbors and friends. I was the one who ended up in prison. Now, I was the one planning to go to downtown Baltimore, to shoot it out with the cops. I was the one who was going to be on the front page of the *Baltimore Sun* for killing all those people. I just couldn't leave her with that legacy. She had not harmed a soul.

*   *   *

An hour later, I shot up some heroin which temporarily eased the pain, and returned to The Block that evening. Christy was surprised to see me and asked, "When did you get back in town?"

"A few days ago, Christy. I was down in Florida, making some serious money, getting high all the time. I'm telling you, it's the place to be, nice weather, sunshine, beaches, and plenty drugs. Why don't you leave with me and go back to Tampa?"

"I can't leave the city. I'm okay here. You need to find yourself a nice girl, and get a job," she countered.

"Look, why don't you team up with me. Peedy Boy won't even miss you after a week. He'll find some other girl." I could see by her expression that it all fell on deaf ears as she was a slave to Peedy Boy. Every time we talked it was the same old thing between us.

Even The Block was boring. Fat Steve and Peedy Boy did all they could to inspire me to start hustling again. They dropped a couple hundred dollars in my hand (which I needed), saying, "Find us some girls, Vinnie."

Needing transportation, I stole a 1980 Chevrolet Monte Carlo three blocks from the downtown police precinct. It had been snowing quite hard earlier. Now the temperature had dropped below freezing, causing major ice spots on the road. I was coming down Bowie Road when the light changed. Off to the right, a Prince George County Police car sat parked in a shopping center. I hit the brakes, and the back end swayed on a patch of ice. Knowing the cop was going to stop me if I ran the light, I tapped the brakes again and begin to slide through the intersection on the red light, clipping a road sign.

My eyes stayed glued to the rearview mirror for the cop. Just as I expected, he pulled out and hit his lights. Without a second of hesitation, I floored it, shooting through two red lights in rapid succession. I pulled out in front by a good margin as the officer had to slow down at both intersections. I ditched the car a block from my mother's house. Running past her place, I glanced over my shoulder to see the cop, stopping next to the Monte Carlo. He began pursuing me on foot in the snow with his pistol drawn.

I ran through several backyards and back out on to the main street trying to lose him. I had to take a chance. I ran between two houses, came around to the backdoor, and busted inside. Five black guys were sitting at a table, playing cards, passing around a bottle of whiskey, wondering what's going on.

I shouted in desperation, "Hide me, man, the cops are chasing me. Please. Hide me."

"Calm down, boy. It'll be all right. Get in that closet."

I stood in the closet like a stone statue with my head against the door, gasping for breath, listening to the black guy talk to the policeman outside. "Naw, I ain't seen no white boy around here."

"Give us a call if you see him."

"Yeah...Yeah. I will."

He came back inside and opened the closet door. "You crazy honkie, what's wrong with you doing something like this. You'll end up getting everybody in the neighborhood arrested."

How was I to know he was running a fencing operation out of his home? It was strange, but that's how I met Willie Goodman. I sat around and drank a couple pints of whiskey with the boys until after midnight.

*   *   *

The word on the street was Willie Goodman would fence anything from a Boeing 727 to a Mr. Coffee. He figured everything had some value. Just to try out our new relationship, I hit a home in Laurel and brought him a small U-Haul of kitchen items, furniture, costume jewelry, and televisions. He was true to his word.

I stole a 1979 Chevrolet Camaro in Upper Marlboro with California plates. Goodman seemed to love out of state cars. He drove it around the block for a test drive like a used car manager of a big auto dealership. He gave me seven hundred dollars.

I told Goodman about a generator at a construction site in Prince George County where they were building a shopping center. The next night we met at the site, and I helped him put it in the back of his truck. We drove to a DC salvage yard and unloaded.

Goodman liked the car thing so much he approached me about breaking into a car dealership in Baltimore County. His boy in New York was starving for some nice, late model cars. He went so far as to rent a car carrier which we parked over in Pumpkin Hill.

I liked the way he was thinking. Let's go for some serious cake. So, I cased the place one Saturday afternoon, and had a good feeling about pulling this off. I called Goodman to make sure everything was lined up, telling him I didn't want to be screwed by the New York boys once we delivered the cars. He assured me the guys were on the level and could handle volume deals.

Goodman and I met at midnight across the street from the dealership. We walked over, popped a rear window, and were sitting in the office in three minutes, scanning through desk drawers and file cabinets. A small security box inside an old Wells Fargo safe had two thousand dollars in cash from Saturday's business, something we didn't expect. I divided it up right there on the spot.

We needed the car titles, which we later found in the safe. The cars would have more value with the titles, especially street value instead of chop shop value. Goodman strolled out to the lot with a piece of paper, wrote down the stock numbers of fourteen cars which he thought would be good sellers. He came back and pulled the keys from the keyboard in the showroom, while I filled out bogus numbers on fourteen different thirty day tags. Hopefully, if a cop saw us driving down the street, he would not be suspicious with a thirty day tag on the car.

About twelve–thirty, we started shuttling cars to The Hill. Half way through, I told Goodman I wanted to stop by my mother's house. I woke her and gave her five hundred dollars. She knew I was up to no good and begged me not to get into trouble. I had a way of telling her not to worry, "Aw, mom, I'm not going to get into any trouble. I thought about all the money I owed you and wanted to bring it by. I want to pay you back for the rental car. Hey, you know I love you."

Goodman was pretty understanding but realized time was wasting, so he revved the engine a few times to hurry me. I hugged her good-bye and was off to steal the remaining cars. I drove the fourteenth car, a 1982 Chrysler New Yorker, off the lot at two o'clock. Goodman drove the thirteenth, and was waiting for me at The Hill.

As soon as I crossed the line into Prince George County on Route 197, a PG cop pulled in behind me. He followed me for three or four minutes as I was in the home stretch to The Hill. Needless to say, I was sweating. I figured he was going to get up on the BW Parkway. Then, he hit the blue lights. I shoved the pedal to the floor before the cop could blink, cut out my lights, and put some distance between us. As I came over the top of the hill, the car suddenly sputtered like it was having a massive heart attack, and ran out of gas. I pulled into the first street and coasted to a stop.

The cop went flying by. From the corner of his eye, he caught a glimpse of the Chrysler. Locking the brakes down, squealing tires, he shoved it into reverse. The engine screamed as he backed up in to the side street beside the Chrysler. I laid flat in the seat, hoping he'd take off running behind the house for me. He ran directly to the car with his pistol drawn and stabbed it against the back of my head. It looked like my luck had run out.

*   *   *

Howard County jail was my favorite…good food, air conditioned, and individual cells. I took the dive and never mentioned Willie Goodman's involvement. Although the detectives knew someone was helping me shuttle the cars, I refused to tell them anything. For the most part, I knew it was all over for me. I sat in my cell, knowing I was going back to The Cut so I prepared myself mentally to deal with it.

Judge McCain was one of the hardest judges in Howard County. I knew he would hit me with the maximum sentence. I stood before him rather lackadaisical as I watched him filter through my records from the past ten years. I could tell he wasn't impressed with my criminal history.

"Mr. Shipe," he said sternly while continuing to read my record.

"Yes, your honor."

"You've got a problem. It seems like the only thing you know is crime. Instead of learning from your first encounter with the system during a four year sentence, you turned that into an eight year stay. You're disrespectful, and making a complete mockery of the judicial system. Some people learn from their experiences, but you have not. I read on your parole hearing where your counselor said, 'You were a detriment to society. He recommended full term on your previous charges.' I understand what he meant." He glared hard at me over his reading glasses waiting for some remorse or defense on my part, but I offered none. "Do you understand me, young man?"

"Yes sir, I understand."

"By the power invested in me by the state of Maryland, I hereby sentence you to ten years in the Maryland adult correctional system with five years back up. The five years will be at the discretion of the parole board after you complete the original sentence."

I looked down and then glanced over to my mom. She was crying with a handkerchief across her eyes. Again, I felt so sorry I had brought more shame and disgrace to her. She was only trying to be supportive of me. Her face was etched with pain and emotion as the deputies accompanied me through a side door to a holding cell.

*　　　　　*　　　　　*

I sat in jail awaiting assignment to the processing and receiving unit at the Maryland State Penitentiary. The stay in Howard County Jail could be as much as ninety days, because of the backup of new inmates in the system. I tried to think through an escape plan in the transfer process. As I recalled from the first time, there were very few minutes of lapse time when anything could be done. Being chained together with three other inmates, alone can be a hassle, but to convince all three to go along with an escape plan would be near impossible.

My mother came to visit me Sunday after church. She told me about a new state program called Excel for drug addicts and offenders. It was a two year program, and she had talked to the director to see if they would intervene in my case. Fortunately, the night I had been arrested, I tested positive for heroin and alcohol.

A week later, I stood before Judge McCain again. He listened to the director asking for my release to the Excel Program, with a promise that if I didn't complete the program, I would be reverted back to serve my full sentence.

Judge McCain appeared not to be interested in how this program could change my life, but he listened anyhow. To my surprise and shock, he began to nod his head, "Okay, okay. This will be the last stop for Mr. Shipe." He turned his attention to me. "Mr. Shipe, do you understand this is your last stop before going back to prison?"

"Yes, your honor."

"I want to make sure you understand that if you don't complete this program, you're going back to serve the full term of your sentence. It will be my recommendation you serve the back up term of five years as well. This court will not show any further mercy or understanding toward you. Is that clear?"

"Yes, sir."

An hour later, I was taken to the therapeutic drug center, where the Excel program was located. I sat in a chair in front of the program's director and two other staff members. They began to ask me a series of questions. "Mr. Shipe, I want you to pretend for a moment, you're out on the Love Boat, hundreds of miles off the coast. You fall overboard. What would you do?"

I thought this was some type of trick question. I hesitated for a minute, "I…I guess I'd call for help."

"Well, why don't you do that for us."

"Help," I said.

"Hey, Mr. Shipe, get the picture. You're out in the Atlantic Ocean. You're getting ready to drown, and the ship is pulling away from you. Nobody would be able to hear you."

"Help, I'm drowning," I said raising my voice.

"We can't hear you, Mr. Shipe? The ship is pulling away."

I raised my hands in a cone around my mouth and shouted as loud as I could, "Help, I'm drowning."

Everyone smiled with a degree of satisfaction, and shouted back, "We'll help you Mr. Shipe. We'll help you." They all applauded as if I had won an Oscar for best actor.

I was convinced from that minute on I was plugged into a pack of loony birds. How was I going to survive two years in this program? I surely didn't feel like I was crazy enough to qualify. To my misfortune, I basically had no choice. I was going to give it my best shot at being a sufferer in order to stay out of prison.

I sat in the prospect's chair with no one to talk to for three straight days, from eight in the morning until eight o'clock at night. Nothing in prison had prepared me for such a difficult encounter. They followed with what they called communication. The staff would enter into the dorm at night and start throwing our clothes, turning over tables, and ransacking the room. Then, we had to put everything back in place, all the while communicating with each other about our task. If anyone was caught not communicating, the entire room would be torn apart again by staff, and the process was repeated.

Next, I was given the patience test. The staff took a cup of water and poured it on to the floor. I was given a two inch piece of cloth and cup, with instructions to mop it up. I squeezed the tiny cloth over the cup to get all the water back in to the cup.

Later, I was given a toothbrush, soap, and a cup of water. My mission was to clean the cracks between the tiles on the floor.

They cut my hair, then shaved my head. A small sign was placed around my neck, like a third grader, saying, "I must learn to listen."

On three different occasions I was forced to sit in the prospect's chair for disciplinary action, until they realized they weren't going to break me. Going back to prison would have been an overall upgrade of my lifestyle compared to the Excel program.

Looking out of a window while I was working in the day room one afternoon, I saw Peedy Boy pull to the front door in his white Cadillac. He reached across the seat and opened the passenger's door. He literally took his foot and shoved Christy off the front seat onto the sidewalk. She appeared to be crying and begging him not to leave her. The staff from Excel helped her inside as he drove away.

It was five days before I had a chance to see her. She weighed only eighty–five pounds, nothing but a skeleton, and only faintly attractive. Her body shook and shivered with the need for a fix as her eyes shifted east and west with a far away look. She and I talked briefly before the staff put her into an isolation unit for another week. It was nearly two weeks before I saw her again. She had put on a little weight and looked much better.

I had to ask, "How'd you like to go to Florida with me, lay out on the beach all day, dance all night, and sleep until noon."

She smiled, and punched me in the ribs.

"Does that mean yes?"

*   *   *

The last straw for me in the Excel program was their verbal reprimand program. A staff member stood at both ends of a hallway and they played me by shouting, "Hey you, yeah you, drug addict. I'm talking to you, boy."

I had to stand there while they chewed me out, "You're walking down this hallway like you own the place. You're a drug addict…the lowest and most worthless piece of human waste on this earth. Do you understand?"

I did everything I could to maintain control, knowing I was getting vulnerably close to going off. After one staff member left, the other one caught me, "Wait a minute, boy. Are you disrespecting the staff here at Excel? For a drug addict, you sure think you're high and mighty."

That was the end of the show. I slammed him up against the wall with such force it knocked the wind out of him. "You punk," I screamed, "I oughta kill you. You don't know who you're talking too, boy."

Quickly the staff subdued me, and took me to the director's office. I told the director as he sat behind his big mahogany desk tilting back in his chair, "I've been here four months, and I can't remember one happy day. I can't remember smiling. I can't remember laughing one time. This is worst than being in hell."

The director cleared his throat as if he were going to give a great speech and said, "Mr. Shipe, there is no hope for you. We can't help you. We can't change you because you don't want to change. There is the door. You've been terminated from the program."

As soon as I left, the director called Judge McCain's office and told him I was dismissed from the program. Judge McCain issued a fugitive from justice warrant against me for violation of a judge's order. An APB was put out for my arrest by the Maryland State Police on September 14, 1983.

*   *   *

Although it may sound strange, I set up camp around the corner from the Baltimore City Police Department. I felt like I only had two choices: working on The Block and going back to robbing on the streets. Peedy Boy was glad to see me. Fat Steve wanted to know where I had been the last six months. Apparently Christy didn't tell them I had been in the Excel program, or about my arrest and the ten year sentence.

Peedy Boy spotted me a fifty dollar bill to hustle some action for him. I borrowed a car and drove out to Laurel. By midnight, I found a girl in an old club of mine, and brought her to Peedy Boy. Just like that I was back in business, hawking in front of the Villanova Club and assisting lonely guys in search of a companion for the evening.

I constantly stayed on the move…spending a night in a motel, a rooming house, or with the few friends I could trust at The Hill. Living on the streets was an expensive lifestyle. Two detectives, Bando and Marley, had me on a fugitive list which they worked. On several occasions, they missed me by minutes.

I stopped by to see my mother one Saturday afternoon, when Bando and Marley drove up in front of the house. I dove out the bedroom window into the backyard and ran down into the basement, hiding in the back corner behind a stack of boxes. It was pitch dark with only a small beam of light coming from the doorway. I could hear Bando and Marley walking through the house searching for me. The backdoor opened and their voices became louder.

I eased my .32 snobnose next to the side of the boxes as their voices drew near. I had not planned a shoot out, but if this was the way it was to end, so be it. I took a series of short breathes to ease my nervousness, and watched the doorway fill with light as Marley's shadow cast an elongated figure across the floor.

The beam from his flashlight shot wildly around in the dark. "Darron, I'm Detective Marley. We saw you go into the house five minutes ago. If you're down here, come on out and let's get this thing resolved. I'll help you. You won't get hurt."

He waited a moment before continuing, "I don't have to come in after you. I can sit out here and wait. Can you hear me?"

I remained silent, wondering if he would really sit out there and wait for me.

"Your mom doesn't want to see you get hurt. She wants you to come on out? You're going to get caught."

I had to make a quick decision, whether I was going to kill Marley now or not. I had been playing tag with him and his partner for nine months. Sometimes I wouldn't hear or see anything of them for weeks at a time, then suddenly they'd show up. They seemed to work my case in spurts.

I sat there scarcely breathing, pondering who I had become. I hated myself and everyone else. If I got killed, got away, got caught, or thrown back into prison, it made no difference to me. What did I have to live for on the outside? I had already spent fifteen years behind bars. Prison was all I knew. I felt trapped by who I was, unable to comprehend what I could be.

I finally decided if he came in after me, I would do what I had to do.

I waited forever while they walked around the yard. Finally, he said, "We're going to catch you, Darron. It's just a matter of time." And he left.

Three hours later, I slipped out the door with pistol in hand, expecting to be ambushed, but no one was there. I sprinted passed a neighbor's house, off into the darkness of the night.

    *   *   *

I sat in my apartment, taking a hit of heroin. A wave of hate and disappointment flooded my mind. The man most responsible for all of it was my father. He was the one who beat me without reason. He was the one who threw my own brother out on the streets at fourteen years old. He was the one who beat my mother almost to death. He was the one who threw my oldest sister out. He was the one who made our house a living hell. It was his fault that all his children grew up inside juvenile facilities or in foster homes.

He was the one person who could never say I love you, or give a hug to show some type of affection. Nobody could live up to his expectations. He would walk right pass me and never speak. Maybe it was because he thought I was his biggest failure. But it was okay, for tonight he was going to die. For all the pain and suffering he had caused everyone else, now, it was his turn. He was going to pay the ultimate price for the way he treated us.

I carefully removed my sawed-off shotgun from the case, and selected five shells to load. I felt good that this day had finally arrived. I had thought about killing my father on many occasions, but never did. If there was anyone who deserved to die, it was him.

As I drove to the house, I thought about the stroke he had recently, and how he suffered partial paralysis on his left side. Why hadn't he just died when he had the stroke? At least mom could have gotten the insurance money. Instead, she had to take care of him.

I stopped in front of the house and left the engine running, because after I blew his brains out I was going to Florida. The door was unlocked so I walked inside, and saw him sitting in his favorite chair watching TV. Mom was sitting on the sofa reading the newspaper. I walked directly over to him and laid the barrel against his forehead, "Sucker, tonight, you're going to die."

His eyes opened a little wider, and I suddenly saw him as a weak, old, frail man...nothing close to the man he used to be. The stroke had stolen some of his speech, and most of the mobility in his left arm and leg. He was pitiful.

My mother dropped the paper in horror and pleaded with me not to do it. I couldn't help but want to ask her, why not? It's for you, I'm killing him. It's to make your life better. It's for all the violence he did to us. Standing up, mom began to cry, and asked me to leave before something bad happened.

I glanced over at her, noticing how old she had become. Her eyes had sunken deep into her head. Her once smooth skin was creased with age lines around her eyes and mouth. All her youthful beauty had been wasted on my father.

My finger eased up and down the trigger with anticipation that he may beg for his life. But he said nothing, not one single sound, which gave me even more incentive. With very little effort, and no remorse, I pulled the trigger, and squinted at the same moment.

The explosion was dead silent. I listened and looked at him at the same time to see he still existed. I ejected the bad shell, reloaded, and fired a second time. Nothing happened again. I ejected the next shell, reloaded, and fired a third time. Silence. I repeated two more times, and still misfired.

The man just would not die. Maybe, he couldn't be killed.

With all the violence and hatred which he had punished others with, the hand of fate had intervened and spared his life. I can't ever remember being more disappointed than knowing he had the opportunity to live another day. Of all the men I had known in prison who had purposely violated the lives of others, my own father was the least deserving to live and breathe another breath.

I dropped the shotgun to my side and cursed him as he sat there staring at me. I took the butt end of my gun and bashed his face numerous times, watching the blood drip over his lips, and the shattered teeth fall from his mouth. I considered it trivial revenge compared to what he had inflicted upon us over the past thirty years. My mother dragged me away, as I continued to curse and swing the gun at his battered face.

Finally, running out the front door, I jumped into my car and returned to my apartment. I stood on the back porch, flustered and angry that I had failed to kill the one person I hated the most in the entire world. Taking the same shotgun shells, I reloaded my gun and aimed at the moon. I pulled the trigger. Pow! It fired, crackling the nighttime silence. Four more times, I jerked the trigger, each time the shots echoed with a loud pop into the night.

Why, why? I asked myself; why hadn't the gun fired when it was next to his head. Maybe the hand of fate was upon me and not him.

CHAPTER 10

I watched her drive into the shopping center parking lot from the door-way of the bowling alley. She was right on time. As I walked out the door, I scanned the area for police cars or undercover agents. My initial thought was she was far too stupid to be a police officer, herself, but by a freak chance, maybe she was followed or under surveillance. For this reason, I had watched the parking lot for two hours before she arrived to see if it was a set up.

I've always liked transactions with amateur drug dealers. They're so easy, and they never report you when they get robbed, except the guy in Tampa, Florida who was the exception and not the rule. I met Susan McCray in a club in Upper Marlboro, which is why I told her to meet me in Laurel, a place I knew she wasn't familiar with. If it was on her own turf, she might have friends hanging close to help her.

She opened the door of her brand new 1983 red Mustang when she saw me cross the street. The car was much more attractive than she was, I thought.

"Like the car," I said, eyeing it from front to rear, glancing around the parking lot at the same time.

"It's a five speed with a 351 Cleveland engine."

I was impressed at her knowledge and love for power. "No kiddin'. I didn't think they were putting Cleveland engines in the 83's."

"Yeah. I drove it off the showroom floor a week ago."

"Business must be good."

"Real good."

"Let me see what you got," I said as she opened the trunk to show me the bag with the dope.

As soon as she looked down, I sucker punched her with a right hook to the jaw. She went reeling in the air like she had been hit by a Greyhound bus, somersaulting head first across the parking lot for ten feet. I reached in her purse and pulled out a wad of cash, which scared me. It must have been over two thousand dollars, plus the two kilos of marijuana in the trunk. This was too good to be true. I was chomping at the bit to get behind the wheel of a Mustang with a 351 Cleveland. As I drove out of the parking lot, she was still laying on the asphalt. A women, who had parked not far away, was walking toward her to offer assistance.

I headed downtown to my apartment, stashed a thousand dollars in the freezer, paid three months rent, and smoked two joints. I just couldn't help myself for wanting to take a ride. I cruised past the Baltimore Police Headquarters in the red Mustang, one hand out the window with the other propped high on the steering wheel, with a .32 snobnose under the seat and three hundred dollars in my pocket. I thought I was as cool as ice. Some of the guys in front of the clubs stared long and hard, finally realizing it was me, and knowing it was a stolen car.

The drive downtown did something for me. Maybe it was the smell of the new car, or being noticed by the guys, but I had a good feeling about myself for just a few minutes. I really thought it was the car as I continued to cruise on Route 1, soaking up the evening air like it was my last night on earth.

Around twelve–thirty, a Prince George County police car pulled in behind me. I knew he was going to hit his lights as I could see him in the rearview mirror calling in the license number. I put a Rolling Stone tape into the player, lit a cigarette, and glanced back in the mirror. Sure enough, the blue lights were flickering like crazy. I stuck my hand out the window, give him the finger, grabbed third gear, and pumped the gas pedal to the floor. The Mustang screamed with a surge, passing two cars in front as if they were backing up. The police car reeled into the passing lane in close pursuit.

I was cranking between eighty–five and ninety, finally able to put some distance between us, when out of nowhere came a second and third patrol car joining the chase. There was not much traffic, but enough to have to maneuver from lane to lane as one of the police cars was quickly gaining ground.

I'm not too sure what happened next. One of the police cars was closing in on my bumper as I slowed to 65 through an intersection, dodging a crazy lane changer. Suddenly, the police car started whirling around like it had hit ice. This slowed the other two patrol cars through the intersection, which is when I really gained distance and pulled out of sight. At least that's what I thought.

Two Prince George County cars formed the first road block. I shot between them like a bullet. The two cops stood on the side of the road and watched in dismay.

I was running over a hundred when I saw the second road block, so I veered off to the shoulder of the road. With dust churning up like a tornado, I smoked through the second road block, fishtailing back on to the road, watching the policeman jump into a ditch to avoid being struck.

Less than a mile away the third road block loomed, which was even more narrow than the previous one. At over a hundred, I shot right down the middle. I could hear sheet metal crying as the police car's bumpers ripped the front fenders off the Mustang. The fenders went flying in to the air like an explosion in slow motion.

The speedometer needle bounced between a hundred and a hundred–ten as I approached the fourth road block about six miles later. I held the pedal to the floor, flying through without any difficulty, probably clearing the police cars by less than an inch.

The fifth and final road block was three miles later. Again, I decided to go down the middle. With only a second to react in steering between the cars, I could see the pathway was too narrow. The sound of the rear quarter panels screeched with contact as I felt an abrupt tug, before the car streaked through with no clearance. I had ran twenty–eight miles, through five road blocks, and was now closing in on DC. I needed to find a place to ditch the car.

I broke into an open stretch, clocking out at a hundred and fifteen. No blue flashing lights were in sight anywhere, when an old man driving a Chevrolet Impala pulled into the passing lane on the opposite side of the road. It all happened in a matter of two seconds, as my speed was so fast that I didn't have time to make an attempt to turn the wheel. He was head on in my lane, traveling forty–five miles an hour, skirting around a U-Haul truck.

The noise sounded like being at ground zero of an atomic bomb exploding. My chest slammed against the steering wheel with such force it felt like every bone in my body was shattered. Pain overwhelmed my body. Glass and metal floated in mid-air in a state of weightlessness. The two cars rose some fifteen feet in to the air as they started to disintegrate on impact. Particles of dirt and dust hovered over the scene as smoke lingers without wind.

Shell shocked, I wasn't sure if I was dead or alive. A loud ringing from the impact repeated over and over in my ears. I realized the Mustang was nothing but waste as it had shrunk to the size of a go-cart. I painfully struggled to escape through the window, rolling over onto the pavement. Glancing toward the old man's car, it appeared to be nothing more than a pile of scrap iron. He sat at the wheel motionless, eyes wide open, like he was frozen in time.

Struggling to my feet, I sprinted to the U-Haul, which had stopped fifty feet down the road. The driver still sat behind the wheel as I approached. I took my knuckle and jammed it behind his neck like a pistol, and said, "Drive or die." He freaked out, and begged me not to kill him.

A county cop with his siren crying slid in front of the truck with his pistol out the window. I couldn't help from laughing as I still had my knuckle stuffed against the driver's neck. I said, "You thought you were going to die tonight, didn't you?" I pulled my hand away. He seemed relieved but didn't appreciate the humor.

I raised my hands to surrender as two cops tackled me and body slammed me to the pavement, repeatedly mashing my face in to the asphalt. I laid face down, handcuffed for five minutes or more while they worked on the guy in the Chevrolet. When they picked me up to carry me to the police cruiser, I glanced over at the old man laying on the pavement as they administered emergency medical care. He looked like he was dead.

*   *   *

At one–thirty in the morning, little did I know that, the Lord Jesus Christ started to put the final plan in action for my life. I stood before the magistrate, who was a short, stocky, older man with thick eyeglasses, sort of geekish looking with a fathead. He tapped on the keyboard of his computer to pull my record. Three pages of outstanding warrants, felonies, and a fugitive from justice warrant covered his screen. He smiled arrogantly at his computer before looking up, "We've got us a good one tonight, boys. This fellow here ain't going to ever get out of prison again." The two deputies grinned like they were holding up a citation bass in a fishing tournament. The magistrate continued, "I'm going to post bond at fifty thousand, Mr. Shipe. I do hope that is too much for you, 'cause I could go higher if I had to."

I told him I thought that would be sufficient.

"The gentleman driving the other car was released from the hospital, so that's in your favor." He looked back at his computer screen, and said seriously, "I can see you've been on the run for a while with all the warrants for your arrest, but tonight, the show is over for you."

The deputies returned me to my Prince George County jail cell, where I awaited a Monday morning preliminary hearing. There was no way out now. I was headed back to prison, more than likely The Cut, a place where I had become accustomed and comfortable. Prison was a perfectly reasonable place for me. The old saying of, 'Three hots and a cot,' a shower twice a week, playing cards, reading pornography, getting high and dodging homosexuals was all I could look forward to in life. One thing I had learned in my short time on the outside was that I hated people; those in authority, those who had an abundance, those who had nothing, and those who wanted to be used. I hated black people, white people, yellow people and mixed people. But most of all, I just really hated me.

*   *   *

Nine o'clock Monday morning, I stood before the judge in a crowded courtroom in Upper Marlboro, Maryland. I now honestly believe, because God had a calling on my life, and was working out the circumstances to get me to where He wanted me, certain things happened. The second of which was in this courtroom.

"Mr. Shipe," the judge said apologetically. "Our entire computer system is down right now." He fumbled through the paper work on his desk, "What are you in here for, auto theft?"

"Yes, your honor. Let me tell you the story. My girlfriend and I had an argument, and in order to avoid any confrontation in public I jumped into her car and left. She called the police. I'm totally embarrassed by this mess. It was a lover's spat. She loans me her car all the time. I just had no idea she would do this."

The judge leaned back in his chair, looking over a police report. "Fifty thousand dollar bond," he said with a strange look on his face.

"That's kind of high. Mr. Shipe, how much money do you have on you, right now?"

"Three hundred dollars, your honor."

"What I'm going to do is set bond at three thousand, ten per cent is three hundred dollars. You post bond and you're free to go, and return to this court April 14th for a trial on the charge of auto theft. Do you understand?"

"Yes sir, your honor."

I didn't dare look back to see if the computers had come on line as I briskly made my way through the door, expecting at any moment for the deputies to grab me. Nobody tried to stop me. I walked directly to the first bus stop, waited ten minutes, and caught a ride to Baltimore.

*   *   *

As always, Peedy Boy and Fat Steve were glad to see me. With the cash I had stashed in my apartment, I bought a thousand dollar car and started hustling out of the Villanova Club. Business was good, four or five hundred a week; some weeks as much as a grand. Before long, I had a pocket full of cash. I'd hawk the front door of the club on Fridays and Saturdays, picking up another couple hundred a night.

To put a damper on things, I knew out there somewhere in the night were Detectives Marley and Bando, crawling around fishing for felons. I had seen the dynamic duo on a couple of occasions, but was able to elude them before they saw me. Someone told them I was working out of the Villanova Club, so I became less visible on The Block. My business simply returned to the suburbs where I broke into houses and small businesses, taking whatever I could carry.

I pulled the car into the driveway next to Willie Goodman's garage and unloaded the goods like a family member moving in. Coming out the backdoor with a strange look on his face, he seemed startled. Willie was quite sure I was doing serious time in the joint for the auto dealership caper. He was thrilled to see me. I told him, "I qualified for an early release program they just started."

"You crazy ___, Darron, you ain't got no early release. You done escaped."

"Come on man, I'm out on good behavior."

"I hear you, but I don't believe you, you crazy honkie."

Whether it was an escape or early release, it made no difference to Goodman. He was a businessman. He sweetened my pockets with cash, and I left for my apartment downtown.

Every time I returned to my room, I had to screen the area to see if anyone was waiting for me. Not only for the police, but I had accumulated many street enemies over the years. I was constantly having to look over my shoulder, trying to see who was eyeing me, who wanted to get even, and who had a hit out. All the years in prison and even after I was released, I could never remember getting a good night's sleep. In the middle of the night if the wind would change directions, I would wake up. My body was constantly fatigued from a lack of rest.

My life as a fugitive had grown old, with never a safe place to relax. Continuously, I was on the run, spending a night here, spending a night there, wondering who had seen me. I read the words 'peace and serenity' in a booklet one day, and it was something I lacked my entire life as a fugitive. I could never seem to find it.

I'd wake up in the morning like a hungry lion, a scavenger, plotting to find a weak person or a place to go where I could turn money. I was beginning to evaluate my animalistic nature and my predatory lifestyle. It was something I couldn't seem to do anything about; it was all I had ever known. It was my game. It was me.

Each day was a new challenge, a new endeavor to stay out of the hands of the law. To remain free, I had to be quick and alert to everything around me all the time, but every good con-man has to possess these qualities.

One evening, I was in a club watching as two girls tried to hustle an older man. I hung close, listening, throwing a few words in their conversation to see if I would fit in to the picture. Neither of the girls was doing exceptionally well. Although, both the girls had been on the streets and knew their way around, the man was merely being entertained.

I bought a round of drinks, and then sat at the table. From that point on I took charge, whispering to the older sister, Shenean, that I could help clean the guy out. At first, she didn't want me to intervene, but after a few more rounds of drinks she liked my game plan as I continued to move things along. I said, "It would look more natural with two couples than with one guy and two girls. Besides, if he tries to get rough, I'll take him out." She whispered something to her little sister, nodding approval to the plan. When the girls went to the rest room, I told the guy, "This girl, Shenean, said she wanted you tonight. What do you say we go party for awhile, and you can drop me and the other girl off somewhere?"

Shenean was all over the guy, like a fly at the dump, when they returned to the table. Her sister, Dinky, sat beside me. We left after a few more rounds of drinks, and stopped at a nearby liquor store. I told him to leave his keys so we could listen to the radio while he was inside.

"Hey girls, this guy hasn't got any money. Fifty or sixty dollars. He's nickels and dimes. Let's ride down the road and get some serious cash, what do you say?"

"He's got a little money. I'm staying." Shenean said, "What do you want a do Dinky?"

"I don't care."

"Shenean," I said, "you're worth more than fifty dollars. Have some respect for yourself. We'll go down to Florida. You can turn a couple hundred a night, easy. Come on, I promise you."

"I kinda like the idea of Florida, but I need some money, now."

"Hey, look, we've got a nice car to drive, I've got a few dollars to get us started. Girl, you ain't seen nothing until we get to Florida. You can dance all night, plenty of drugs, and sleep until noon. Who wouldn't want to do that? Come on, what do you say?"

"All right, Vinnie, all right, let's go," Shenean said. "But if I don't like it, are you going to drive us back?"

"Of course, I'll drive you back. But there's nothing not to like about Florida. Money everywhere. You girls will do fine."

"Vinnie, where are we going to stay?" Dinky asked.

"Nice places. Like the Floridan, the Hilton. I've got friends down there to help us."

"I like the sound of that," Dinky said.

I jumped behind the wheel, cranked it up, and squealed out of the parking lot. I glanced in the rearview mirror, catching the guy coming out of the liquor store, and raising his hand in desperation. I threw my hand up to say good-bye, as I pulled on Route 197, heading south.

Shenean knew a drug dealer in DC who sold us two hundred dollars of heroin and a couple pints of booze. By the time we hit I-95 South, we were out of it. My mind was jello, as I set the cruise control on fifty–five, holding the right lane in light traffic leaving Woodbridge, Virginia. Somewhere around Fredricksburg, I started to make sense of things again.

Going past the Ladysmith exit, a Virginia State Police car was posted on the ramp. He eased in behind me, and tailed me for about a mile before flashing the blue lights.

I turned to Shenean and said, "I'm going to make a run for it, hold on." She said, "Go for it, Vinnie! You're the man."

Of course, I wasn't sure if she knew there was a state trooper behind me. I kicked the big Buick hard, and shot past a couple of cars, which dodged out of the way of the flickering blue lights in pursuit. The chase was on for the next twenty–six miles with speeds up to hundred–fifteen miles an hour.

*   *   *

The two tractor trailers, who had been monitoring the chase on their CB's, set up the middle lane to pinch me. The second I approached within fifty feet, the tractor trailer in the left lane drifted to the middle lane. I had to tap the brakes to slide to the left lane, then he shot back in the left lane, forcing me into the median.

When the car first flipped in to the air, Dinky grabbed my arm and held on with all her strength. The car hit the ground with a bounce, and was back in the air, twisting like a steel trapeze act. Shenean was thrown from the side window as if she was a rag doll. The car hit the ground again, ricocheting a third time, continuing to rotate in the air like a carnival ride, losing no momentum. Again, it rolled and leaped into the air a fourth time, landing upside down in the north-bound lane of traffic, sliding south.

The sheet metal screamed with a hideous high pitch as it scraped across the concrete highway. The noise was unbelievable. The view was unimaginable, like sitting on the front row of a movie theater upside down. Cars were heading straight for us, trying to swerve and dodge the out-of-control vehicle. Some cars came within a few feet of hitting us as we continued to skid towards the oncoming traffic at incredible speed.

Four hundred and seventy–five feet later (the distance of one and a half football fields), the cream colored Buick came to rest in the middle of Interstate 95 north-bound lane. I had cheated death once again. Gasoline poured from the tank onto the pavement as I climbed through the window. Cars slowed down, squealing their brakes, as the state police cars drove across the median. An air of chaos reigned.

I dashed toward the woods, running at full speed while people watched, not sure what to do. Two state troopers gave chase on foot. I ran even harder, pushing myself to the limits. Let them shoot me in the back, I didn't care. I gasped for more air, finally seeing a little distance between us when my feet went out from under me. I had stepped in a hole, and laid sprawled on the ground. Before I could get to my feet, the two troopers wrestled me to the ground and handcuffed me.

Traffic backed up for miles into Henrico County. There were ten to twelve state police cars with blue flashing lights brightening the night sky. The Richmond TV news team filmed the scene, the upside down car, and me in the back seat of the police vehicle. As miraculous as it was, I overheard the state police tell the news reporter, one of the girls had been thrown out the window, and only had suffered a broken arm and bruised ribs. The other girl in the car had received a broken foot.

Rather ironically, miles away a Godly woman was watching the eleven o'clock news which reported the chase and the wreck. The Spirit of God fell on Pat Hale and she dropped to her knees and began to pray. "God, please intervene in this young man's life and do a miracle; change him to be a minister of the gospel of Jesus Christ. You, God, are greater, wiser, more powerful than all of creation. Would You make a way to use this man to your Glory?"

Little did Pat know, God had His work cut out for Him.

*   *   *

I was first booked in the Hanover County Jail. Uniquely enough, the chase started in Spotsylvania County, through Caroline County, into Hanover County, and the car slid a hundred feet into Henrico County. Technically, all four counties had jurisdiction. Somehow, they sorted it out in Spotsylvania that the charge was speeding; in Caroline and Hanover counties the charges were of fleeing and eluding, both felonies; and Henrico dropped charges because the chase wasn't inside the county line. On top of that, the state of Maryland filed an immediate fugitive from justice warrant with an additional eight felony warrants. Boy, the new paperwork was piling up fast!

I was locked in an area called J Block of the Hanover County Jail. My days were spent playing cards and watching a TV mounted on the wall at the end of the catwalk.

Every Friday, Cowboy Bob and two other volunteers, visited J Block. They came to the corner of the catwalk, sang, and talked to us about Jesus Christ. The singing was all right, but I didn't care much about the preaching. When Cowboy Bob said something to me one day, I informed him, "There are two things I don't like, cowboys and God, so bug off."

Cowboy Bob continued to visit, always stopping by my cell wanting to talk to me about Jesus. I tried to ignore him, and sat in my cell reading. He would stare at me sometimes, and make me feel extremely uncomfortable.

L. D. MORRIS
CLERK

ALBERTA M. MORTON
JULLIET BOONE
DEPUTY CLERKS

CLERK'S OFFICE CAROLINE COUNTY
BOWLING GREEN, VIRGINIA 22427

January 2, 1986

Dear Mr. Shipe:

In total there are six (6) Warrants Of Arrest as follows:

7 April 1984   Failure to stop for a police officer
                after being given a proper signal, namely
                siren and flashing lights, etc.

7 April 1984   Operation of a motor vehicle in a reckless
                manner at a speed of 115 MPH in a 55
                MPH zone.

These two Warrants were issued by Trooper F.T. Melson.

7 April 1984   Failure to stop and give aid and information
                after being involved in an accident in-
                volving property damage (Hit and Run)

7 April 1984   Driving under the influence of alcohol, hit
                and run, reckless driving, eluding Police
                Officer.

7 April 1984   Operation of a motor vehicle without a valid
                operator's license

7 April   Operation of a motor vehicle on the public
                highway in a reckless manner, to wit: en-
                dangering life and limb.

These four (4) warrants were issued by Trooper M.P. Monroe

Mrs. Norma L. Polley, Deputy

One Friday, while I was playing cards, Cowboy Bob walked over, and said, "You know, Jesus, is the answer to all your problems. He's the one you've been running from all your life."

I interrupted, "Look, I don't believe in Jesus. I don't believe in God. I'm an atheist, now leave me _____ alone." I continued playing cards, but I could feel him still staring at me. "What's your problem, man? What are you staring at?"

He shook his head as if not understanding my answer, "Son, I've never met a man in a situation like yours who didn't believe there was a God."

"Well, now you have, so bug off."

Cowboy Bob continued to hang around so I went to my cell and got a cup of urine which I threw in his face. He looked back at me with the most compassionate eyes. Dripping wet, he said, "Praise God, Jesus bless his life. Bless him, Lord. Open his heart to know You."

From then on, every Friday before Cowboy Bob and the volunteers entered, I was locked down in my cell so they could talk to the other inmates. Still, I heaved cups of urine at them if they came too close. I couldn't understand why they continued coming each week. They were relentless, determined, and fanatical. Although they said very little to me after that, I couldn't help but listen as they shared the gospel. They talked about Jesus like He was their next door neighbor.

Three months later, I was transferred to the Caroline County Jail, leaving Cowboy Bob and his disciples behind. It was there that I planned my escape.

*   *   *

It was Saturday afternoon and Soul Train was on TV. I had prepared myself by exercising, putting on my running shoes, and shadow boxing in the corner. My main objective was to get hurt bad enough to be sent to the hospital. I would try my escape, either upon arriving at the hospital or when being treated. Everything would depend on the setting and the guards.

About six or eight of the blacks guys had gathered by the TV to watch the girls. A real loud guy by the name of Chucky Willis was in the middle of the group, whooping and hollering as the girls danced. I walked over to the TV and turned the dial to some channel, where a country and western singer called Porter Wagoner and The Wagonwheels were singing in front of a campfire.

"Hey man, what you doing changing the channel?" one of them shouted.

"That's Soul Train, you turned off, man," Chucky said.

"What's wrong with you?" Another said in an angry voice.

I stood by the TV, looking directly at Chucky, "You don't like it?" I knew he would react to the statement, especially because he had five or six home boys hanging around him.

Chucky turned, shouting to master control, "We got a crazy cracker down here, man. Need to get him out of here."

"Don't call for help. We're watching what I want to watch," I said, hoping to stir someone up for a fight.

"You ain't right, man." The guy beside Chucky said. "Everybody wants to watch the girls, instead of a bunch of cowboys sitting around a fire."

"Turn that channel back to Soul Train, Chucky," another said.

The guards rushed in and my whole plan was foiled before it ever got off the ground. Two guards grabbed me, forcing me into an isolation cell in another unit. I exploded with anger as my scheme fell apart.

Every Friday, an elderly man named Mr. Gravitts came into the cell blocks to preach. Unfortunately, I had to listen. Even though my cell was at the end of the block, his voice carried through the entire unit. Several times, he walked past and wanted to speak to me, but I told him, "I'm not into the religious thing, just leave me alone." After cussing him out, he didn't bother me anymore.

One afternoon as Mr. Gravitts was praying at home, God spoke to him through Matthew 25:35–36 NIV "For I was hungry and you gave me something to eat, I was thirsty and you gave me something to drink, I was a stranger and you invited me in, I needed clothes and you clothed me, I was sick and you looked after me, I was in prison and you came to visit me."

After reading this, he fell down on his knees and asked the Lord what He would have him do that day. The Lord directed him to go to Caroline County Jail and visit Darron Scott Shipe with a message from God.

*   *   *

I found it difficult to function in the Caroline County Jail. Every one was awakened at six o'clock, forced to wear orange jumpsuits, and required to perform daily tasks for general maintenance of the facility. It was too militaristic for me. For not participating, I was sent to the isolation unit, which was fine with me. I could care less about the general welfare of the facility. The days passed slowly, but it was something I had become accustomed to through the years. I was still awaiting extradition back to Maryland for the charges on the stolen Mustang, and assault and battery. The new charges of auto theft with the Buick were now pending. Then, I would have to go before Judge McCain for re-sentencing on grand auto theft, robbery, and breaking and entering for the auto dealership. Plus, I had no idea what other charges might arise when I returned to Maryland.

All total, I was in a bad situation. The only thing I could see ahead was spending the next twenty or twenty–five years in prison. I had no hope or future. I was at the end of my rope. I had to resign myself to the fact I was inmate 132534A…and that's all I'd ever be. (An *A* behind one's number was to designate a returning inmate.)

Looking out the window one afternoon, I asked myself, will there ever be any hope for me? Will I ever be free again? Will there ever be a life for me beyond the walls of an institution?

In all my years in prisons, I had been able to control the depression and mental torment, which sometimes resulted from hopelessness. I was able to block it out, but the load was finally getting to me. I had lived a wasted life, without purpose, without reason, and now I was having to pay the price. My family was ashamed of me. My, so called, best friends were not around. It was just me having to live with me, and I didn't like what I saw.

At that hopeless and depressing moment, Mr. Gravitt cautiously peeped around the corner of the cell block. The guards had warned him of the violent rage I had been in earlier. He approached my cell, "Darron, can I talk with you a minute?"

I told him to come over, I'd talk with him. He stopped at a distance in the middle of the gangway. I could smell the scent of fear on him as he began to share how God had a purpose for everyone's life.

"I came today," he declared in a stronger voice, "to tell you God said this morning you're not going back to prison. You'll be coming back into the prisons, but you'll come in to preach His word, of how He can set a man free on the inside. You'll be a testimony for those who are without hope, and those who have given up on life."

The words shocked me at first. I didn't know what to say. "Look, there's no hope for me. I've already been sentenced to ten years with five years backup. I'm going to prison. I'm just sitting here waiting to be transferred back to Maryland. Come back and talk with me when all this is over."

Mr. Gravitt's voice became soft and compassionate, "I don't believe it, son. When God says something, He means it. I don't believe God wants to put you back into prison for the next ten to fifteen years of your life. Will you pray with me about it?"

I watched the old man ease closer, using the bars to lower himself down to his knees in a prayer position. "Yeah, I guess so," I said, as he reached through the bars for my hand, closing his eyes and praying like he believed every word he spoke.

I was glad it wasn't a long prayer. I couldn't even remember what he was praying about, except for my eyes to be opened to the power of God and His calling on my life. Nothing happened as far as the supernatural nature, but for the first time in my life I felt peace. Whatever was to happen to me was no longer in my hands. The show was in God's hands now. Although I was quite skeptical, I never mentioned anything to the old man. Mr. Gravitt said, "I'm going to contact a program called New Life For Youth, which can help you."

Two weeks passed before Pete Puig, the assistant director for the program, came to visit. Pete asked to see me, but the guard told him I was about to be transferred to Maryland, and I was destined to spend my life behind bars. The guard asked him if he would like to visit with another inmate. Pete seemed surprised. "No. I want to talk to Darron Scott Shipe."

The guard told him to be careful because of my violent nature, but agreed to let him in for a visit. As soon as Pete saw me, his eyes began to water. He was grieved in his spirit for me in the small isolation cell with only a two inch foam mattress to lay on. He fell down on his knees in front of my cell and immediately broke into tears. He said he had never been in prison and he didn't know what it was like, but for twenty years of his life he had been a prisoner of heroin addiction. He rolled up his sleeves and stretched both hands inside between the bars so I could see the needle marks on his arms. He said he had been set free for over seven years now and was living a victorious life in Christ. Only a God of mercy and grace could do something that miraculous.

I told him of my situation, and how I was awaiting extradition back to Maryland to serve my time. Realistically, there wasn't much hope for me.

He said, "There wasn't much hope for me either, until Jesus Christ came into my heart and changed me into a new man. Jesus can put hope back into your life wherever you go."

I reluctantly told him I wasn't sure there was a God. I was an atheist, but if he still wanted to pray to his God, I would agree with him.

Through a stream of tears, he smiled, and said, "I wasn't sure there was a God either until He set me free from heroin seven years ago, and now I know. Let's pray. You're about to see how powerful my God is." He said sixty men at the ranch would be praying for me every day. He reached under his Bible and gave me a copy of a book, *The Son Of Evil Street*, by his pastor, Victor Torres. He said Victor had been a gang leader and a drug addict in New York, who had started a program for people just like me.

After he left, I felt like maybe there was some hope. Every night before I fell asleep, I read the book, prayed, and called out to Pete's God of hope, "Help me, God! If You're out there somewhere, let me know. I'll serve You all the days of my life. If You can give hope to a drug addict in New York, use him, and make him a respectful man, why not me?"

*　　　　*　　　　*

Two detectives from Prince George County picked me up and carried me back to Maryland to stand trial on the auto theft charges for the Mustang. The prosecutor wanted a jail sentence of at least three years plus restitution for the car. But I was about to see God intervene in a powerful way, which got my undivided attention. Judge Woodman asked the prosecutor, "How much does an inmate make a day for working...eighty cents? You can garnish a third. At that rate for thirty–six months, the victim would only receive $292 toward the payment of the vehicle. Let's go with restitution, placing Mr. Shipe on three years probation to pay the amount in full."

To my surprise, the prosecutor agreed with the terms. Somehow, hoping, I would be able to pay off the car in the next three years, I guess. No one ever asked me if I had a job. The truth was in my thirty years, I had never had a 'real' job. The only skill I had was the ability to rob and steal.

I was taken to a holding cell to be shipped to Howard County for a court date with Judge McCain. I knew this would be the end of the road. Strangely enough though, I had an unexplained peace, and all this really didn't matter to me anymore. I continued to read the Book of John and prayed each night for God, somehow, to work all this out to His glory. The remoteness of the first court's decision on restitution with no jail time was rather unusual, maybe even a divine intervention, I thought. Knowing, beforehand, the reputation of Judge McCain as a hard judge with very little compassion, I knew God would have His hands full dealing with him.

As silly as it was, each day I read over again, the brochure about New Life For Youth, which Pete Puig had given me. On the front was a picture of four or five guys sitting on a tractor, seemingly happy, smiling, and waving, which I thought was kind of dippy. A bunch of jerks riding around on a tractor didn't fit my bill for a good time. But the more I looked at the picture, the more I hoped that someday, I could be on that tractor…being happy, smiling and waving.

Pete Puig had sent to my attorney, Louie Shaw, all the documentation explaining the New Life Program. Louie stood in front of Judge McCain, telling him they had several hundred graduates who had completed the program, and today were successful people and attributes to society. She pleaded with Judge McCain to consider the option and give me another chance.

Judge McCain listened, but he didn't listen. Finally, he interrupted, addressing me, "Mr. Shipe, my opinion of you is that you're a worthless good for nothing bum, and you belong in prison. You belong behind bars." He reached for my paperwork, and continued, "Everything we have attempted to do for you, you have spit back in our faces. You have spit in the face of the judicial system. You have spit in the face of our programs. You have personally spit in my face. Less than a year ago, you stood in this very court room, and I listened as you asked for the chance to enter the Excel program. I gave you a chance. Four months later, you quit, and spit in their face. Then you go out and get more charges on top of what you already had. And you come here today wanting me to send you to this New Life For Youth program? I'm not going to do it."

Judge McCain took my paperwork, tore it up, and threw it over his shoulder on to the floor. "You're a bum. You're just a bum. You don't want help. You just want an easy way out of everything. I'm not going to give you an easy way out this time. You don't want any help. You don't deserve it." Judge McCain was thoroughly disgusted. He stared hard and long at me, before looking over to the state's attorney. "What does the state recommend?"

The prosecutor rose slowly from his table, "Your honor, in all due respect to what you have said, let's give him one last chance. If he messes up again, we'll give him the fifteen years, plus there'll be new charges. I'm sure we can find charges to add on top."

Judge McCain leaned back in his chair with his fingers intertwined together in front of him. "Today is October 18th. I'm going to take seven days to consider the state's recommendation. I'm personally going to find out about this New Life program. On October 25th, all parties will return to this courtroom and I'll render my decision at that time."

*   *   *

On October 25, 1984, Judge McCain granted his final approval for me to enter the New Life program, but warned me sternly, "If you don't make it, there will be no more chances. You will go directly to prison."

I went back to jail and waited. The voice came over the intercom, "Inmate 132534A report to center hall with bag and baggage." I could not believe it, so I waited to hear it a second time, "Inmate 132534A report to center hall with bag and baggage." I grabbed my toothbrush, toothpaste, underwear, and socks and stuffed them into a paper bag. I walked briskly to center hall, knowing something supernatural had happened in my life.

My mom met me at the front gate and drove me to the bus station. I could hardly believe it; I was a free man. I wanted to celebrate. While my mother was taking care of my ticket, I slipped out the back door of the terminal to go get high.

I stopped in to see Peedy Boy and Fat Steve, and shot up heroin in an alley with a friend. I hung out with him for awhile, but a small voice kept telling me to return to the bus station that this was my last chance. I finally left and walked back to the station, only to see my mother sitting alone in the corner crying her eyes out. I was always the one who hurt her the most. She hugged me, and begged me to catch the next bus.

"Mom, I'm okay. I can make it," I pleaded with her, but she continued to cry.

"Son, this is your last chance, don't you understand? If you don't do this, you'll never have another chance. You'll spend the rest of your life in prison."

"I'll get a job, I don't need this program."

"Like the judge said maybe you don't want any help."

She hit a sensitive nerve. Even in my obliterated state, what she said was true. Maybe I didn't want any help. "Okay mom, okay. I'll catch the next bus."

I caught the 8:40 out of Baltimore to Fredricksburg, Virginia. Mom stood next to a wall, with tears in her eyes, waving good-bye. I ended up in Richmond, as I passed out and missed my stop. Pete had been waiting for me in Fredricksburg and thought I'd bailed out on the program. I called the New Life ranch and told them I missed the stop and would be coming in on a later bus.

Just before three in the morning, I stepped off the bus and Pete greeted me. "God bless you my brother," he said, rejoicing, maybe even surprised, I had made it. "We serve a powerful God, of mercy and grace, and He has shown His mercy upon you."

We got in his car and drove to the Ladysmith exist. It was like de ja vue, where everything started and everything would end. We drove in the country for miles, until we reached the ranch. As soon as I opened the door of the car, I heard the of silence of the country. I stood there for a moment looking up into the clear, starry sky. The heavens were peppered with tiny dots of God's creation. All my life, on the streets, on The Block in Baltimore, and in prison, I was surrounded with noise. Never had I enjoyed quietness and the beauty of a million stars. It felt like a foreign land.

It was early fall when the leaves had started to turn, and nature had begun to die, but I felt alive with hope. I had a peace which surpassed all understanding, something I had never experienced.

At eight o'clock in the morning, we made our way to the recreation room for prayer. Although I didn't quite understand it, I went along with the program. After breakfast, we had morning Bible Study for an hour, then satellite teaching from a college in Dallas, Texas for three hours. The afternoon was filled with chores and special assignments by the staff.

Most of the men seemed sincere in their commitments. However, I was caught somewhere in-between, attempting to grasp this relationship with Jesus Christ, and playing the game of words which sounded good. Being a good con artist, I learned the lingo and the right words to say, but I'm not sure I fooled anyone.

I struggled with my old nature from the first day I arrived. While out on the porch, one of the guys came up and said he loved me, kissing me on the cheek. I hit him square in the mouth, but was quickly restrained. Pete came and tried to explain the guy didn't mean anything out of line. It was merely a Christian way of expressing to me that he didn't care about my past. He cared for me now like a brother. It was the same love that Jesus had for me.

In the afternoon, everyone gathered outside in a big circle for a time of prayer with Pete and his wife. I kept my eyes open watching the people as they prayed, wondering what kind of loony bin I had entered. Someone said, "I want to thank God for our new brother, Darron Shipe. I want God to bless him and open his heart to the length, depth, and height of the love of Jesus Christ that surpasses all knowledge that he may know and understand the power of God." Two or three others chimed in, "Thank you, Lord, for brother Darron."

That night, I broke into a cabinet and stole a couple of candy bars as if it was a big caper. I followed up two nights later cleaning out the entire cabinet. I looked for something to steal like a drug addict in need of a fix. Most of the items were worthless things Willie Goodman wouldn't buy.

About a week later, I had a fight with some guy who thought I reminded him of his uncle. I pulled him outside behind a shed and beat him. I had my hands wrapped around his neck, strangling him, when one of the staff members came and pulled me off. The guy fell to the ground, gasping for air. I was called into Pete's office to explain what had happened. He told me from now on to pray before I hit anyone. I promised I would try to abide by the rule. It was something I had never done before, so it could be difficult. It was more natural for me to hit, then pray.

*   *   *

Richey Arriaga was a Puerto Rican gang leader from Bronx, who had been in the program for a month. He was a mass of skull tattoos and gang news. Jose Polonco was a gang-banger from Brooklyn, who at one time contested for boxing's Gold Gloves Championship. We lifted weights together in our free time, and I listened as they gave their testimonies of how Jesus Christ had changed their lives. None of it really registered with me, but I listened to what they had to say.

In our Sunday morning church service, I was sitting on the front row between Richey and Jose. We had a wide screen TV in the day room. A special evangelist, who everyone was looking forward to hearing, was coming on at noon. I had never heard of him, so it made no difference to me. This man's message was about the crippled man sitting at the temple gates…a man who was on the outside and missing out on what God was doing on the inside. He was nothing but a poor beggar, like all of us, deprived of the knowledge of Christ. He was spiritually crippled, burdened down with the cares of this world, and carried around aimlessly by his friends and circumstances.

I listened off and on, as my mind drifted from downtown Baltimore to Tampa, Florida. The evangelist made an altar call for anyone to accept Jesus Christ and surrender his life to Him. It had a strange effect on me and caught my attention. The TV camera picked up an old bum coming down the aisle, crying at the top of his lungs, "I'm just a bum. A nothing. A nobody. I'm worthless."

The words danced across my mind, loud and clear, echoing as Judge McCain's exact words, "You're a worthless good for nothing bum. You're a nothing." The words cut like a knife, deep into my heart. I watched the bum make his way down the aisle. It could have been me, I thought. The evangelist kept telling him as he came forward, "Today, you're being adopted as a child of the King. God doesn't care what you look like. He sees your heart, your inside. Jesus is going to set you free, my friend. He doesn't care about your past, only your future."

I tightened my lips, watching to see what happened, as the bum made his way down the aisle. People cleared a path so he could move closer to the altar. "I'm tired, Lord," he cried. "I can't keep going any farther. I don't deserve anything." That was me.

The evangelist reached out to grasp him, "My brother none of us deserve anything, but it's by His mercy and grace we're set free. We're not going to get what we deserve, but we're getting unmerited favor. How many standing before a judge would want justice for their crimes? How many would want mercy for their sins? Give me mercy any day."

I was in a zone, so focused and zeroed in on this man, who was me. It was the way the judge saw me, the way the world saw me, and the way God saw me. And it was the way I saw myself for the first time. I was nothing in the eyes of man.

The evangelist announced he was going to lead everyone at the altar in a salvation prayer. I listened intently to every word as I began to repeat the words in my mind with the pastor. When I said the words, "Jesus have mercy on me a sinful man," I instantly felt something happening inside me. With Richey on one side and Jose on the other, I knew I couldn't cry. They all knew what a tough guy I was, and I'd look weak in their eyes. After I looked down on the parquet floor, I saw three or four tears in a small puddle, which I tried to hide with my foot. Oh God, I thought, I don't want to cry in front of these guys. Please don't let me cry. Please.

All the time I was asking, "Jesus come into my heart. Please forgive me, because I'm a nobody, a bum. Nobody loves me, but if You love me, come into my heart. I'll live my life for You."

I was doing all right, holding back, until big old Richey laid his arm around my shoulder, gave me a squeeze, and said, "Go on, and let go. Jesus is talking to you. He wants all of you, Darron. All of you." The bottom fell out and the tears rolled down my face in buckets. I couldn't stop crying, as Richey's arm held me tightly. Jose reached over and patted me lightly on the back of the head. I knew right then I'd been forgiven of all my sins, and set free. For the first time in my life I was crying, and it felt good. It was cleansing, just like the blood He shed for my sins at Calvary. At that moment, I felt the love of Christ going to the cross and dying for my sins. I felt His love which surpasses all understanding of laying down His life for mine. He died so that I may live.

I stood up and boldly announced to the men, "I've been set free, guys. I've been set free, today. Praise God Almighty, I've been set free." I was hardly able to contain myself. At last, the scales of unbelief had been removed from my eyes. I ran outside and sat under a big oak tree, gazing around like a little child. I saw for the first time what a beautiful world God had created. All the trees had the most beautiful colors. Who, but God, could create something as wonderful and magnificent as this? The birds were singing and dancing on the tree limbs, glorifying and praising God. White fluffy clouds rolled slowly across the deep blue sky like snow sliding down a waterfall.

Many of the guys were still in the day room when I returned. I looked at God's marvelous creations, the Puerto Ricans, the blacks, and the whites with love. Real love. I realized they were truly my brothers in Christ. They were each a special creation from the God who rescued me. It was Jesus Christ dying for my sins, and me accepting the free gift of salvation that had set me free. All the pain, destruction, violence, and crimes I had committed were no longer charged against me. As 2 Corinthians 5:17 KJV says, "If any man be in Christ, he is a new creature, old things are past away, behold, all things are new."

On November 11, 1984, the former inmate 132534, with no hope, without a future, died to Christ, to never live again. I, Darron Scott Shipe, was that man.

Chapter 11

Serving God wasn't easy, because all my life I had been programmed for hate, violence, and destruction. Now, suddenly, I was to replace it with love, peace, and joy. Constant warfare captivated my mind...a struggle between my old nature and the new nature in Christ. From the onset Satan lied by telling me I wasn't saved and I was only kidding myself about salvation.

Ephesian 6:12 NIV says, "For our struggle is not against flesh and blood, but against the rulers, against the powers of this dark world and against the spiritual forces of evil in the heavenly." The battle for my soul was in the spiritual world, in a place where I was not used to fighting. God's Word told me, "The weapons we fight with are not the weapons of the world. On the contrary, they have divine power to demolish arguments and every pretension that sets itself up against the knowledge of God, and *we take captive every thought to make it obedient to Christ.*" 2 Corinthians 10: 4–5 NIV. This meant I had to take control over my thoughts and keep my mind on Christ. Slowly I was understanding the power of prayer and staying focused on God.

I was attempting to draw closer to Jesus, but each day I fought the old man's nature of wanting to go back to the streets, get high, or lash out at someone. My flesh begged for more attention, calling out for me to feed it like I used to do. Not sinning was like being a heroin addict going into withdrawal.

Temptations were constant, but I resisted and stayed with my commitment to Christ. I wanted to break loose of the bondage of slavery to sin I had lived in for thirty years. I had tasted the good life of the new relationship with the Creator of the universe and was indebted to Him for what He had done in my life. The divine power of a living God had intervened through circumstances and events.

By society's judgment, I should have been back in prison serving time, but Jesus Christ had mercifully set me free. I needed to trust Jesus every day with my new life which He had given me. This was very difficult because I had never trusted anyone my whole life. Con's are programmed to mistrust people, and keep an eye always open.

"Darron you need to grow and become strong in the Word," the counselor said. "God's Word gives us wonderful promises and assurances for the new life. Your maturing depends on learning the Bible, which is your food for spiritual growth. You need to eat, live, and breathe it every day. All of God's promises and assurances are to be received by faith through His Word."

I needed to believe that God's Word had divine power to change me. Even if I didn't understand it all, I needed to study, meditate, and pray over His Word, so it would work faith and obedience in my life.

As easy as all this seemed, I brought a lot of baggage with me. I was an ex-con with an attitude problem, a mistrust problem, and a hatred problem. Eight years of prison life just doesn't wash away in a few days. I was trying to learn God's way of life instead of my way. I was sincerely striving to walk in the spirit, but I had a lot of the old man in me and struggled daily.

Bible classes started at nine o'clock in the morning and lasted until twelve. Lunch was from twelve to one, and from one until two was prayer time. Sixty former drug addicts, gangbangers, robbers, thieves, and criminals would enter the dayroom and seek God for one solid hour. Angel Cruz, the director, and Pete Puig, his assistant, cried out for God's help and mercy to remake us and mold us into men of God. Every man was a broken piece of clay on the potter's wheel to be molded and shaped into a new creature in Christ.

*   *   *

A short time after arriving at the ranch, I received three assault charges. Each time, I was summoned to the office before Angel and Pete and sternly warned of the fifteen years plus which were pending in the court system. They prayed with me and cried out to God to help me with my violent nature and the prison mentality which I still possessed.

On one occasion, Pastor Victor Torres came to the ranch and talked about the problems of violence. It was my first time meeting the man I had read about, and it was obvious he had the immediate respect of all sixty men. Everyone got the message he was a no nonsense man, who would not tolerate any violence or discord at the ranch. He had a unique ability to reprimand with love and compassion, while having the respect of every man in the facility. He was like the Godfather of miracles; the ex-drug addict and ex-gangleader role model, who proved there was a God. And so were Pete and Angel for that matter.

His wife, Carmen, spoke a week later at an evening service in the day-room. She was a powerful woman of God with a strong spiritual discernment. She had no idea who I was and had no knowledge of my background. She walked up to me, placed her hand on my heart, and said, "You're going to be a peacemaker."

At first, I didn't put much credence in her statement. I had definitely never been a "peacemaker" and I wasn't sure if my violent nature was controllable, even though I believed God could do all things. But my doubts were so strong that I believed that this was something I might have to live with as a Christian for the rest of my life.

*   *   *

At eight o'clock each morning, we began our devotional with someone opening with a scripture and a short message. In my third month, I was given an opportunity to share with the group. I spoke on Hebrews 10:26 NIV: "If we deliberately keep on sinning after we have received the knowledge of the truth, no sacrifice for sins is left." Not only did God give me a strong message for the group, but it was a heavy message for me. The staff came over and complimented me on the presentation. God truly was working in my life.

A short time later, God began a series of miraculous events. I was shuttled up for court appearances in Prince George and Howard County. In each case, I saw God move in a great and powerful way. One after another, the judges made favorable decisions to the charges and the payback of restitution. I gave God the glory, witnessing to my lawyers and probation officers of what had happened in my life.

My mom, and sister Charlotte, came for a visit. They both realized something drastic had taken place. I preached to both of them for several hours on the saving grace of Jesus Christ. Mom had seen thirty years of my failures and now, for the first time, she saw hope. I was sold out on this new life in Christ and I didn't care who knew it. I thought it would be best to start with my own family first. I wrote my brother, sister, aunts, uncles, cousins, with little or no response from any of them.

One evening, I called Christy and told her how I had accepted Jesus Christ and had been set free of the old lifestyle on the streets. She seemed overwhelmed: "Vinnie, that's good for you. I'm so glad you've changed."

"Christy, Jesus could set you free, too, and make you happy. Just try it. I beg you to see how God can change your life around. I'm going to send you a Bible. Start reading the book of John to find out how real Jesus is."

"Fine, send me a Bible," she said half-heartedly.

"I guarantee you'll get peace, joy and love. Jesus is the answer, Christy. This is what we've been searching for all these years; I'm not kidding. This is the real thing!"

"Okay, Vinnie. Okay."

"It's Jesus Christ. He's alive and He'll do for you what He's done for me."

"Look, I…I gotta go, Vinnie. Don't forget to send the Bible, okay?"

Quickly, I sent a Bible off to Christy, and prayed for her salvation, expecting almost immediate results. A week passed before I called her again and shared my heart, begging her to at least give it a try. I wrote her a letter, and shared how God was working in my life and how I wasn't the same man I had been six months ago. She wrote back with a lot of small talk about how happy she was to see I had found peace in my life, but the religious thing just wasn't for her. That was the last time I ever heard from Christy.

Slightly dejected over her failure to read the Bible, I sent a mass mailing to my friends and inmates about my recent conversion to Christ. Only two or three people wrote back, and none seemed to be interested in changing their lives. I had prayed, and obediently sent out the word with no interest from anyone. There was a wall of isolation being formed out there against me. It was almost like I had a disease. Only God knew how hurt I was, because I needed a friend. I felt so lonely and rejected.

*   *   *

I struck up a conversation with a girl from Philadelphia who came to visit her boyfriend in my dorm. We hit it off quite well as friends, sitting around talking most of the day. When she returned to Philly, she showed my picture to her friend Barbara. A week or so later, I received a short letter from Barbara telling me about her life. I wrote back and told her a little about myself, and how Jesus Christ had changed my life. We exchanged letters for several months, and then I didn't hear anything from her.

Philippines 1:6 NIV: "Being confident of this, that he who began a good work in you will carry it on to completion…." As I had surrendered myself, body, soul, and spirit to Jesus, I now had confidence that He would take care of me and provide for me, "…according to His riches in Glory."

I knew my faith would be strengthened by seeing what God could do in my life: "We were chosen, having been predestined according to the *plan of him* who works out *everything in conformity* with the purpose of his will" Ephesian 1:11 NIV. I could be assured He had everything under control for my life. God's plan was slowly coming into existence right before my eyes.

After a long silence, one day I heard from Barbara. I was surprised, because it had been four or five months, and I assumed she had interests other than writing to me. I wrote back and told her of the Victory Celebration we were having at the ranch, and invited her and her girlfriend to come. She accepted the invitation.

From the first moment she arrived, we knew God had placed us together. We took a walk on the grounds and she said, "I needed to tell you something. God gave me a dream, and told me I would be marrying a man who had been in prison." This seemed totally out of character for this college graduate with a strict religious background.

"That's interesting," I said. "I'm looking for a good Christian girl to spend the rest of my life with." We both laughed, knowing God had put us together.

The upper photo is
Barbara and I after
our wedding. The
lower photo is at
the New Life for
Youth Ranch, several
months after being saved!!!

After graduating from the New Life Outreach program, I went to Pennsylvania to ask Barbara's parents for permission to marry their daughter. Not quite sure how I would be received, I trusted God in this situation to work everything out to His glory. Barbara had prepared the family the best she could about me and my past. But even with the best of preparations, my reformed life as a criminal concerned a lot of people.

*　　　　　*　　　　　*

Starting out married life was a struggle. Never having a job was a distinct disadvantage, but I knew God would provide. At the recommendation of church friends in Richmond, Virginia, I was hired to work in a lumber yard. God used the owners to bless me by purchasing a car and allowing me to pay them by the week. I worked hard and diligently as unto the Lord every day, always trying to be a testimony of God's grace. After six months, I was appointed foreman and given substantial raises.

When Barbara and I applied for a mortgage loan for a house, we again saw the power of the living God. The mortgage loan officers wanted three years of income and tax records which, naturally, I did not have. I told them I could only provide six months. Three weeks later, our home loan was approved.

On weekends, I did small jobs, like building sheds or inside repairs. When God told me to go into business for myself, I knew this was the next step in my faith walk. I proceeded to the county to obtain a business license. I was immediately refused, because of a felony conviction. After much prayer and supportive letters from people who knew me, three weeks later the initial decision was overturned. I made up five hundred flyers, and started walking door to door looking for business.

Finally, I got my first customer. An old grandmother called me from down the street to come to her house (actually, she thought I was the mailman). I ran over with great anticipation, realizing God had given me my first job. I could almost count the dollars of blessings.

She took me inside and showed me her rocking chair. The slats had worn loose, causing the chair to wobble. I scurried out to the car, got my glue, wood screws and a hammer and fixed it up, just like new. She gave me ten dollars, and I walked out the door praising God for his faithfulness.

Food was scarce on our table at times, but we were learning to have faith and trust God. At our weakest hours, a check would come in the mail or a job would materialize to give us food and mortgage money. David in Psalm 37:25 NIV said, "I was young and now I am old, yet I have never seen the righteous forsaken or their children begging bread." I can attest to this scriptures being true in my own life.

I built my first room addition in an upper middle class neighborhood in Chesterfield County. From that job, and the recommendation from the customer, I began to build a reputation as a reliable general contractor with a high standard for workmanship and excellence. I've maintained that reputation for the past fifteen years. Starting with residential business, I later was awarded large commercial contracts for apartment complexes throughout the Richmond area. I renamed my company Masterpiece Remodeling to give praise to God. All of this was an example of how God rewards those who diligently seek Him and serve Him.

Sometime later, Barbara and I were invited to the ranch to share with the men about God's faithfulness. As I was walking around talking to different people, I noticed a man staring at me. His face was familiar, but I couldn't place him. As he became more and more conspicuous with his long hard stares, I edged closer to see if I could remember him.

Finally, I stood in front him, and we looked at each other, not saying a word, for several seconds. He could tell I wanted to cry as he strained hard into my watery eyes. His eyes became glassy because he thought he might know me.

"Do you know me?" I asked.

"Yeah, I think so, I'm not sure," he said with an emotionally tight voice. "You're Cowboy Bob, aren't you?"

"Yeah."

"I'm Darron Shipe, who was in the Hanover Jail. I threw urine on you, remember? I told you I was an atheist."

"Sure, I remember. I told you I've never met a man in your position who didn't believe in God."

"Cowboy Bob, I'm saved, and serving God everyday of my life. Jesus saved me, Cowboy. Jesus saved me."

We embraced with a hardy hug. "Praise God, Darron. Praise God!" He cried grasping for words. "God really does answer prayer, doesn't He?"

"Thank you for coming in and sowing the seeds of God's word in my life." I turned around and said, "Cowboy Bob, I want you to meet my wife, Barbara."

"God has been good to you, Darron."

Barbara showed Cowboy Bob a picture of our children. His face lit up with surprise and delight, examining the photo like a spiritual grandfather. He walked away, patting his eyes with his handkerchief, praising God for showing him he had not labored in vain all those years in the Hanover Jail.

*   *   *

Barbara and I drove up to Baltimore one Saturday afternoon, parking around the corner from the Villanova Club. From the moment we entered the club, loud pounding music, a feeling of uncleanness, and a spirit of oppression prevailed in the air. The young girl standing in the doorway had crude black curls over her head as though she was experimenting with adulthood. She wore a snug thin red cotton dress three inches above her knees, with a matching deep heavy rose colored lipstick. The strong smell of cheap perfume caught my senses by surprise, as I asked for Fat Steve.

Never before had I felt the spirit of evil and demonic control until I entered this place with the spirit of the living God in my heart.

Instantly, there was a war of good versus evil all around me. I was determined I had to do this. I had to come back to the streets where I lived and share the freedom I had found in Christ Jesus.

Fat Steve smiled when he saw Barbara and me. "So good to see you again," I said as he stepped out of his office.

He chewed the last bite of a hot sausage, gulping it down, "Vinnie, Vinnie, I haven't seen you in a couple years. Are you ready to hit the streets again?" He said eyeing Barbara as if I was bringing her to Fat Steve. "Plenty of money on the streets, honey."

"Let me tell you, Fat Steve, something great has happened in my life."

"Good, good, Vinnie," he interrupted.

"I've accepted Jesus Christ as my Lord and Savior." I blurted out. "I'm living a holy life, pure and clean. He set me free of a life of sin and destruction, Fat Steve. I felt like I needed to tell you this."

His face fell down several inches as he searched for words to say. "Well, that's great Vinnie. That's what you needed."

"A relationship with Jesus Christ is what we all need. It's the only way to be set free from sin." I watched Fat Steve feel the discomfort of God's calling. It was not my idea to come see him, but I'm not sure he understood how the Holy Spirit sends people to witness and share with other people. God, surely, has an appointed time for each person to hear the gospel message so that no one will be able to stand before a great and mighty, perfect God, and say, "No one told me about Jesus Christ. No one came to me and shared the gospel message of salvation."

"It's great seeing you again, Vinnie, I'm glad things are working out for you. Peedy Boy opened a small sandwich shop in town. I haven't seen him in awhile. I've got a lot of things to do." Nervously, he patted my shoulder before making his way back to his office.

"God bless you, Fat Steve," I said as he closed his door.

There was a degree of finality seeing him walk away, ignoring, putting off, not receiving any hope of eternal life. His heart had hardened with the cares of this world, nothing else was of interest to him. Even when the day of accountability was fast approaching, he could not see beyond the doors of the Villanova Club. A short time later, he had a stomach stapling operation, loss several hundred pounds, fell ill, and died in a Baltimore hospital.

*　　　　　*　　　　　*

Every Monday, Tuesday, and Thursday night, I return to prison...the place God said I would return to be a testimony of His saving grace and divine mercy. Sharing with the youth at the Bon Air Juvenile Correctional Center has been a pure blessing of God's faithfulness. I tell the young boys and girls that if they accept Jesus as Savior now, they won't have to go through the hell and misery I had to endure.

This was taken at the Bon Air Juvenile Correctional Center. I had the opportunity to speak to over a hundred boys at an outside concert. This defies all odds of mere coincidence. God said I would return to prison to preach the gospel. Lower photo is Rick Conner and I going in for Monday night Bible Study.

Christmas morning of 1998, Rick Conner and I walked from cell to cell leaving a Christmas goodie bag of chocolates and a Bible with each of the inmates. (Rick Conner invited me into Bon Air Juvenile Correctional Center in 1997, fulfilling God's promise of returning to the prisons as a witness). We spent a few moments with each kid, sharing that Jesus Christ was the answer to all their problems, and that He cared for them on this Christmas morning.

As I stared into the eyes of a young twelve year old boy, I saw myself thirty years earlier...sitting all alone in a juvenile facility on Christmas morning with no family visit, no one to hold me, and no one to tell me they loved me. The overwhelming loneliness and emptiness began to eat into the pit of my stomach, as I noticed his eyes brimming with tears. He looked fragile and scared. I wished I could have hugged him and held him like a loving, caring, father, but it was not possible.

When I handed him a Bible, he said softly, "Thank you, sir, for coming to see me this Christmas."

The guard slammed the solid steel door shut. I said, "Jesus is the answer, son. Just Jesus. He did it for me, and He'll do it for you." He pressed his tearful face against the glass window as I walked away. I could feel his stare for the longest time.

Rick and I went to the parking lot and cried.

          *   *   *

In January, I received a letter from a young girl in Bon Air Juvenile Correctional Center: "What you said really touched my heart. I don't remember but a few Christmas days when I was out. I guess cuz there was nothing special to stand out in my mind, but the normal traditions. This year was my sixth Christmas locked down and it meant more to me than any Christmas in my life. I've never seen anyone (except staff who had to) come out here on Christmas day. It really meant a lot to us to see you, but to see Jesus working through you also...The gifts you all brought were so much more than what was in the bags, it was the gifts from your heart.... You bring me hope. I always feel like there's no future after here. I guess you felt the same many times, but you show me there is hope and that I can make it if I trust in the Lord and walk with Him.

"A lot of things you say remind me of my life. I got locked up at 12 and grew up in the system. I missed out on all the normal teen-age activities, i.e. dates, proms, school, and things of the sort. But even though I missed those things, I often feel I have gained so many more valuable life changing lessons missing it all and being here.

"I look at you and know one day I can go out there and become someone because you did. I've read plenty of books about people changing and making something of their lives after prison, but you are so much more real in my life than they are. I believe them, but I see you. I'm sure you know the difference.

"I always think, that all I'm going through and the time I'm spending here, that if I can just take that and change one person, and help just one, that it will all be worth it. I just want you to know that you have helped one and gave one a lot of hope."

*   *   *

God holds out His promise of hope to anyone who will believe. It is the hope which will give you strength to overcome any mountain you may be facing. It is the hope, that you are no longer alone, and the situation you're in can be resolved by God Almighty.

I'm eternally grateful for Pete Puig of the New Life Outreach Ranch, who came and spent one hour with me sharing the gospel. The man who stretched his arms between the bars and convinced me there was hope. Pete died in the fall of 1989.

My mom continued to live in Maryland. She had the pleasure of seeing me change my life around and start serving the Lord. In her final days, she was proud to see me make something out of myself and become successful. In fact, one day she read a letter I wrote to her from prison about that very thing: "One of these days you'll be proud of me. Just wait and see."

With tears in her eyes, she said, "I am son. I'm really proud of you." The last three years of her life I drove to Maryland every two weeks to spend the weekends to cut her grass, do small chores, and take her out to dinner. She would come and spend a week with me during the summer. She died of cancer in March 1996. I had the pleasure of standing by her graveside one bright sunny afternoon preaching her funeral, sending her home to meet her Savior the Lord Jesus Christ. She finally laid her burdens down to receive her rewards in heaven.

After his second stroke, my dad lost most of his mobility and speech, and was confined to the house. I visited and told him how I turned my life over to Jesus Christ. I shared the gospel of how all have sinned and come short of the glory of God. I apologized to him that I was not the son growing up that he was proud of, and I asked him to please forgive me. He said he would. He later accepted Christ as his Savior. During his final days, I sat by his bed for hours reading the Bible, feeding him meals like you would a little baby, and dabbing his lips with a napkin.

Just before he died, I laid next to him on his bed, and said, "I forgive you, dad, I forgive you. I really love you from the bottom of my heart."

He closed his eyes and drifted off. I leaned over, kissed him on the cheek for the last time before I left, and whispered, "Goodnight dad, sleep well. It's just between you and God now."

Driving back to Richmond, all I could do was cry and hum that old song, "Amazing Grace, how sweet the sound, that saved a wretch like me; I once was lost but now I'm found, was blind, but now I see."

My Final Thoughts to You

As I sit here completing my story, tears are flooding my eyes, dripping down onto the pages of this manuscript. The things which I used to do in order to live in the world and survive inside prison overwhelms my heart with sadness and disbelief. God forgave me for being so foolish, risking my soul for an eternity in hell. This may well be the case with you right now.

2 Corth:5:17 KJV says, "If any man be in Christ he becomes a new creature, old things are passed away, all things are new." This is an example of God's faithfulness. My old criminal nature is passed away. My old life of sin is gone.

My story shows that all things are possible with God. If you allow Jesus Christ to enter into your life, even if you're a man like myself without hope, or just a person who is aimlessly wandering through life without direction, He can give your life meaning. But it is only by surrendering and committing your life to Him that you become a new creature. Open your mind and heart to live for Jesus each day, making the decision that you don't want the life you now have. Make the decision that you want what God has for you.

God is real. It's doesn't matter who you are or where you are, what you're about, or what color you are, what creed, what you've done in the past or what you haven't done. God can change you. He can give you a new start in life, but only if you want it.

There is a story in Mark 10:49 NIV about a blind man sitting on the side of the road, calling out to Jesus for help. Jesus stopped, and asked him, "What do you want me to do for you?" The blind man said, "Lord, that I can see." Jesus responded by saying, "Go. Your faith has healed you."

Are you blind? Are you sitting by the roadside, and going to let an opportunity of eternal life pass you by? Maybe you're blinded by believing you're a good person, by being religious, or attending church. But do you really know Jesus Christ? Do you have a personal relationship with Him? If you were to die in the next five minutes, would you know where you would spend eternity?

A leper came before Jesus, knelt down and said, "Lord, if you are willing, you can make me clean." Jesus reached out his hand and touched the man, "I am willing, be clean." Immediately, he was cured.

Jesus can touch your life right now, if you're willing. If the leprosy in your life is sin and separation from God, He's there for you. If your life is without hope and a future, He will make a way for you. If your life is filled with hate and violence, He will show you love and mercy. If you are willing to take the step of faith and ask Him to make you clean, He is willing to give you a new start in life.

Would you pray with me?

Dear Jesus, I haven't been honest with myself or anyone else. I'm a sinner who needs help. I'm like the blind man who needs to be able to see. I'm like the leper who needs to be clean. I beg You to forgive me of my sins and give me a new start in life. Please come into my heart and fill me with your Holy Spirit. I promise to live my life for You and serve You all the days of my life. Thank you Jesus for saving me. Thank you for turning my life around. Thank you for giving me a second chance. Amen.

Contact Darron S. Shipe for services and schedules

Darron S. Shipe

New Life Outreach

5745 Orcutt La.

Richmond, VA 23225

804-276-6059

For the next book in the *"From Crime to Christ Series"* contact:

Visit our web site: http://skyboom.com/agapegangsters

Rick Conner

Books may be ordered at Barnes and Noble, Border Books, and Amazon.com